PURSUIT

For Kim,

I hope you enjoy the continuation. This is my favorite

Jacline O

Visit us at www.boldstrokesbooks.com

By the Author

After Dark Series

PURSUIT

by

Jackie D

2017

Credits
Editors: Victoria Villasenor and Cindy Cresap
Production Design: Susan Ramundo
Cover Design By Sheri (graphicartist2020@hotmail.com)

Acknowledgments

Thank you to the Bold Strokes team, for turning my ideas into readable stories. Especially Vic Villasenor and Cindy Cresap for helping fill in all the missing pieces. Thank you to my mom for always reading and for pointing out any and everything that was missed. Thank you, Alexis, for telling me to go upstairs and write, and to keep writing. Last, but not least, thank you to all the readers that are pulling for Brooke and Tyler, it has allowed me to continue their story.

Dedication

For my wife, it's still you—it will always be you.

Chapter One

Two sets of footsteps echoed through the abandoned, inadequately lit alleyway. Tyler could feel her chest burning from the exertion, but she was rapidly gaining on the figure in front of her. Eight other targets had been eliminated in the last hour, but this was her primary objective. It'd be the icing on the cake. She pumped her arms, willing an extra burst of energy to erupt through her legs. The figure took a sharp right around a corner, and suddenly, the footsteps halted.

Tyler froze. She backed against the wall and moved the last ten feet on high alert, trying to mute her ragged breathing so as not to give away her exact location. She squatted and used her gun to clear the corner the figure had just darted around. Nothing. No movement, no noise. *You can't hide from me. I'm coming for you.* She moved back to her side of the wall and waited. She counted to three and took the corner again, this time pushing forward to the abandoned pallet leaning against a Dumpster. Tyler knew the person was on the other side. She could sense it, feel it in her bones. Her heart pounded, adrenaline surged, and she couldn't help but smile.

The Dumpster shifted slightly. Tyler leapt around the corner and came face-to-face with her conquest. She managed to take aim before her target had the opportunity to, which put Tyler in control. The target wasn't expecting it, and her expression said so, clearly. She held her hands up in the air and laughed, shaking her head. Tyler beamed back. This was her favorite part of the hunt, when the prey was out of options and backed into a proverbial corner. She placed her finger on the trigger and pulled with no hesitation and no regret. The shock was plain as she looked down at her chest where a glowing red light started to pulse.

"Just had to pull the trigger didn't you, Monroe?"

Tyler holstered her weapon and shoved her shoulder as she strode past her, almost skipping back toward the training entrance. "Just making sure I get my points."

Caden Styles was quickly beside her. "When are you going to give in and finally agree to play on my team?"

Tyler patted Caden's shoulder. "As soon as you catch me."

Caden rolled her eyes. "You know I let you win, right?"

"Ha! Whatever helps you sleep at night."

The other agents taking part in the training exercise had already left the facility. It seemed it was always Caden and Tyler that remained. Tyler briefly wondered if they were subconsciously playing on the same team already, pushing everyone else out to toy with one another.

They walked over to the monitoring station and waited for their scores to print. Caden's flopped out first. She grabbed it and started poring over the numbers. She gave Tyler a sideways glance as she read her own. After a few moments, Tyler folded up the piece of paper and put it in her pocket.

Caden lifted an eyebrow. "Aren't you going to tell me your score?"

Tyler shrugged and turned toward the locker room. "It doesn't matter what I got." The smile she felt forming on her lips probably came off a bit more smug than she intended.

Caden rolled her eyes. "You got a perfect score again didn't you?"

Tyler pulled off her vest and hung it on the rack that was located just outside the double doors of the training facility. "You did too…minus catching me, of course."

Caden pulled off her vest and removed her training weapon from its holster, then handed it to the agent behind the desk. "Sure. It's the *minus catching you* part that's starting to piss me off."

Tyler smiled. "You're still coming over for dinner tonight, right?" They went through the large double doors and into the locker room.

"I'm only coming if Brooke is making lasagna."

Tyler shook her head. "I'm cooking."

"Then no. I have a pretty steadfast position on knowingly poisoning myself."

Tyler shrugged as she pulled off her shirt and replaced it with a plain black one that didn't have Homeland Security printed across the chest. "Have it your way. More alcohol for me."

Caden matched Tyler's movements and grabbed a shirt out of her bag. She smelled it and cringed at what Tyler assumed was an unpleasant odor. She tossed it back into her bag and pulled out a sweatshirt, repeating the smell check process. This piece of clothing seemed to meet her basic requirements for cleanliness, and she pulled it on. "I'm a better friend than that. I wouldn't ever want to imagine you having to drink alone."

Tyler pushed the door open to leave. "So noble."

❖

Brooke was putting the last of the groceries away when she heard the front door close. She shut the fridge where she'd just placed the last of the beer and came out of the kitchen to greet Tyler. It still surprised Brooke in simple moments like these how disarmingly attractive Tyler was. The fact that Tyler seemed to have no idea how gorgeous she was only intensified the effect. Her eyes were still as blue as the day they'd met a little over a year ago, though they were calmer now. Some of the pain had subsided, and there was often peace shimmering in her steely blues. Her smiles were more frequent, and her demeanor had settled in a way that made Brooke's heart melt.

Tyler placed her gym bag on the floor and wrapped Brooke in a warm hug, her blond hair tickling the side of Brooke's neck. Brooke kissed her quickly, and Tyler smiled. "How was training this morning?"

Tyler's eyes brightened when she spoke. "It was awesome!"

Brooke laughed and kissed her again. "I take that to mean you beat Caden again?"

Tyler wiggled her eyebrows. "I did, but just barely."

Brooke playfully smacked Tyler on the backside and went back into the kitchen. "You two are so competitive it's scary."

Tyler followed her and took a seat at the kitchen table. "I'm not sure you're really in any position to judge competitive nature."

Brooke feigned shock, placing a hand over her heart as Tyler continued.

"I don't think I know anyone more competitive than you, Brooke Hart."

"I'm not competitive. I just like to win."

Tyler stood and closed the distance between them, grabbing Brooke again and pulling her close. "It's cute you think there's a difference."

Brooke kissed Tyler's chin, working her way around to a spot right below Tyler's ear that she'd discovered quickly led to Tyler's undoing. "Cute, huh?" Brooke loved the way Tyler's arms tightened around her. Tyler made her feel safe and loved. It wasn't until she'd met Tyler that it even occurred to her that these aspects were missing from her life.

"Did I say cute?"

Tyler's speech was starting to slow as Brooke continued near her ear. "I meant unbelievable sexy."

Brooke raked her teeth down the column of Tyler's neck. "You taste salty."

Tyler pulled Brooke's shirt up and ran her hands up and down her back. Brooke couldn't control the shiver that followed Tyler's fingertips. "Since when did my sweat bother you?"

Brooke continued to kiss her neck. "It doesn't. I'm simply thinking of all the things I'd like to do to you in the shower." Brooke pulled Tyler's shirt over her head and started leading her backward toward their bathroom. Brooke's phone rang, and Tyler groaned in disappointment. Brooke kissed her slowly, then patted her cheek. "Go get in the shower, and I'll meet you in there in a minute."

Tyler grabbed her gym bag and walked toward their bedroom. "You have five minutes, or I start without you."

Tyler disappeared into the bedroom. Brooke smiled and pulled her phone from her back pocket, sliding the green answer button after she checked the Caller ID. "Hi, Jen." Jennifer Glass sounded like she was in a crowded area.

"Brooke, hi. I was just calling to see if you needed anything before I head over?"

Brooke opened the fridge. She glanced over the food before she answered. "No, I think we're okay. Thanks for checking, though."

Jennifer mumbled something under her breath that was directed at a passerby before she continued. "No problem. Is Agent 'I'm better than everyone else in the world' going to be there?"

Brooke rolled her eyes and smiled. "I believe Caden will be here, yes."

Jennifer let out a long, dramatic sigh. "Fine. I guess I'll deal with her to spend a day with you, Tyler, and Patrick."

Brooke started toward the bedroom, anticipating Tyler's body under her hands. "Very sweet of you." She could hear the smile in Jennifer's voice when she responded.

"Make sure you start the rumor I'm sweet. I need more adoring fans. Okay, I'll see you guys in about two hours, then."

Brooke pulled her shirt over her head and placed the phone back to her ear before speaking. "Sounds good, see you later, Jen."

Brooke ended the call and tossed the phone onto the bed. She stripped off the rest of her clothes and headed for the bathroom. Steam was rolling like fog from behind the glass door, and she pulled it open and stepped into the shower, already aroused by Tyler's naked body before her, glistening from the spray of the water.

Tyler's smile widened as she moved over to let Brooke into the hot water. "Was that Jen?"

Brooke pushed her hair back into the water. She could feel Tyler's eyes on her as she let the water wash over her body.

"The one and only." Brooke turned around to face the spray. Tyler moved up behind her and placed her arms around her waist as she began to kiss Brooke's shoulder.

"I'm surprised she's waited a whole week after we moved in to come over."

Brooke leaned into Tyler, placing a hand on Tyler's head to pull her closer. She closed her eyes, savoring the feeling. "Work has been a bit crazy."

"Mmmm." Tyler was clearly done with the conversation as she slid her hands over Brooke's stomach.

She felt Tyler's hand run down her center, and desire started to thunder through her body. Brooke grabbed Tyler's other hand and squeezed. Brooke's need was bordering on painful. Her nipples tightened under the hot water and Tyler's scorching embrace. Tyler's hand drifted lower, gently sliding between Brooke's legs. "That feels so good." Tyler pulled her closer, pushing her hand lower and deeper into Brooke. Brooke's breathing increased, and small moans began to escape the back of her throat.

Brooke was familiar with the burning sensation growing in her belly, but she wasn't ready for climax. She wanted this moment to last as long as possible. She wanted Tyler to be exactly where she was, to feel what she was feeling, simultaneously. She grabbed Tyler and pushed her back against the small blue tiles of their shower. Brooke knew that she loved to be possessed, taken. Brooke pinned Tyler's hands to the cold tiles as she nibbled and nipped her way down Tyler's neck and chest. She slowed when she reached Tyler's nipples and pulled on each one with her teeth, giving enough pressure and pain to elicit an approving growl. Brooke moved back up Tyler's body until she reached her mouth, kissing her hard. She released one of Tyler's hands and put the other one between her legs. Brooke took her hand and pushed between Tyler's legs. She continued to increase the pressure on her clit as she watched Tyler's eyes change. They were turning hazy and heavy. Brooke bit down on Tyler's shoulder, needing to be closer. The heat and slickness around Brooke's fingers drove her orgasm closer to the edge, and when she felt Tyler begin to pulse around her fingers, her last string of resolve snapped. Wave after wave of sheer pleasure consumed her as she moaned Tyler's name. Tyler quivered under her, and Brooke loved it. Loved that she could put her in this state and loved that Tyler trusted her to do so. After several minutes, Brooke kissed Tyler's smiling mouth. "Get out so I can wash my hair. I can't concentrate when you're standing there looking at me like that."

Tyler kissed her one more time before pushing the glass door open. "I'm going to take that as a compliment."

Brooke smiled at her. "You should, Special Agent Monroe."

CHAPTER TWO

Tyler opened the windows in their bedroom and took a deep breath. The air was full of warmth and springtime. It shouldn't have been seventy-two degrees in the middle of April in Washington DC, but it was. She looked through her drawers, excited to wear shorts, something she hadn't planned on being able to do for at least another month. After she dressed, she went into the bathroom to finish getting ready. She could hear Brooke singing along to the radio and smiled. She'd never felt so content, so at home, or so loved in her whole life. She checked her watch and hurried to the backyard to get things started.

Tyler lumped the coals together on her new grill. Her aunt Claire had given it to them as a housewarming present, and this was the first time she'd be able to put it to use. She meticulously lit each corner and watched the hump of black squares ignite. Satisfied with her progress, she grabbed a beer out of the fridge. There was a knock at the front door, and it swung open before Tyler had the opportunity to get across the room. Caden sauntered in carrying a six-pack of beer and wearing her ever present cocky smile. "I didn't interrupt anything, did I?"

Tyler laughed. "Are you asking or just voicing wishful thinking?"

Caden opened the fridge, pulled out a beer, and popped open the top, and took a long pull from the bottle. "No one wants to see you naked, Monroe. Don't flatter yourself." She smiled and took another sip out of the bottle.

"That's not true." Brooke pulled Caden into a welcoming embrace.

Caden kissed the side of Brooke's cheek. "I said no one wants to see Monroe naked. I didn't say anything about you, Brooke."

Brooke shoved her in the chest, squeezing Tyler's hand as she passed toward the kitchen.

"You have quite a way with women, Styles."

Caden shrugged. "Brooke doesn't count. She has some weird Tyler force field up, making her immune to my charms."

Brooke smiled. "Why don't you two do me a favor and get out of my kitchen? Go play outside." She winked at Tyler.

Tyler held up her hand in the direction of the sliding glass door. "Age before beauty."

Caden grunted as she passed. "I'm only two years older than you, Monroe."

Tyler smiled. Getting under Caden's skin was something of a sport, one she loved to play.

Caden let out a long whistle when she stepped into the backyard. "This is awesome!"

Tyler stood next to her. "It's one of the reasons we picked this apartment. It has somewhat of a backyard."

Caden nodded. "I'll say! You have a full patio set and a fire pit. Hopefully, we get to use it tonight."

Tyler checked the coals. "I don't see why not. It sure is nice enough out."

Caden pulled out a chair and sat down. She pulled her sunglasses off the top of her head and slid them on as Tyler took a seat next to her. Caden turned and looked inside before she spoke. "Have you talked to Brooke about Lark yet?"

Tyler watched Brooke move around the kitchen bobbing her head to the Pink song that blasted from the speakers, her cutoff jean shorts accentuating her youthful twenty-six years, as opposed to the suits she had to wear every day at work that made her look older. "No, not yet."

Tyler let her mind wander back to when she had first met Brooke. In actual measured time, it had only been a year, but their experiences through the minutes, hours, days, weeks, and months made it seem much longer. Brooke had always been strong willed, determined, and focused. But she had also been a bit idealistic, youthfully hopeful. That is, until she discovered one of her classmates had been working against her agency and the country right under her nose. She was blissfully unaware of the evil that hid in the shadows of people's subconscious minds, bathed in blood and revenge. Nathanial Lark, Chris Carlson, and Michael Thompson had stolen that from Brooke. They had ripped that light from her eyes, the light that Tyler would have given anything to return to her. But Tyler knew all too well that you can't unring a bell, and no number of kisses or promises could reaffirm a sense of security that never really existed. This was the burden of the protectors, and Brooke was now a protector.

Caden took another sip of beer. "You'd better, before Glass opens her big mouth."

Tyler leaned her head back against the chair, pushing away the dark thoughts dancing through her mind. "What is it with you and Jen?" She was trying to change the subject, and Caden let her.

"There is nothing *with us*. She drives me crazy, and I try my best to return the favor."

Tyler fought the urge to smack her shoulder. "She's one of Brooke's best friends, so do you think you could tone down the jerk thing, at least for today?"

Caden finished her beer and set it on the table. "I can try, but it just comes so naturally." She smiled widely.

❖

Jennifer Glass could hear the music booming from outside the front door. She decided to push it open instead of knocking, and she was glad she did, or she wouldn't have been able to stop and watch Brooke dancing around the kitchen singing into a beer bottle. Jennifer thought back over the last two years. Brooke and Jennifer had never been enemies per se, but they weren't as close as they were now. There'd been fierce competition between the two of them while they trained together as computer analysts at Camp Peary. Well, the competition was probably more on Jennifer's part, if she were truly honest with herself.

Brooke seemed to excel innately at everything she touched, while Jennifer had to work for everything she accomplished. Brooke was naturally beautiful, and she had a glow about her; Jennifer thought of herself as rather plain. Brooke was athletic and incredibly physical; Jennifer had needed to put in dozens of extra hours to pass the hand-to-hand combat training course Tyler instructed. Brooke had the ability to put people around her at ease, to help them feel secure; making friends for Jennifer had always been a challenge. She sighed. It didn't matter where they'd come from; they were here now. They were friends, and Jennifer would do anything for Brooke.

Brooke glanced in Jennifer's direction, and her face lit up. Brooke had a way of doing that, making you feel as if you were the only person in the room that mattered. Brooke practically tackled her with a hug, and Jennifer laughed. "Where'd that come from?"

Brooke pushed Jennifer's hair out of her eyes and tucked it behind her ear. "I'm happy to see you. I got used to seeing you every day, and it's been over a week."

Jennifer kissed her cheek. "I missed you too, weirdo."

Brooke grabbed her hand. "Let me give you the grand tour!"

The apartment was exactly what Jennifer had expected of Brooke and Tyler. The main living area was very open and airy, the dark leather couches and dark entertainment center screamed of Tyler, whereas the pale green walls and feminine art was all Brooke. The guest bedroom had been set up as an office space with a bed. One wall was covered in books that ranged from murder mystery novels to tech specifics for computer systems. The computer station had four screens, which was typical for Brooke and Jen's line of work. The adjoining wall was covered in pictures of Brooke and Tyler's life together. Their compatibility showed in each image of bike riding, hiking, and the beach. Several images included Patrick and Jennifer, and then in equal measures, Caden and Tyler donning all-black battle gear and holding a variety of weapons. Jennifer followed Brooke into the bedroom. "I can't believe how quickly you got everything set up and unpacked."

Brooke seemed to think about it for a moment. "This is the first real home Tyler has had since she lived with her aunt as a teenager. I wanted her to feel settled."

Jennifer smiled at Brooke's answer. She was always thinking of other people's well-being. Jennifer was grateful to be on the receiving end of that kind of consideration.

The master bedroom was impressive. It had hardwood floors like the rest of the apartment, and an entire wall covered in alternating glimmering white and black closet doors. The bed frame and end tables were the same white color as the closets. The adjacent wall was a bright blue that made Jennifer envision the Caribbean Sea. Another wall was covered in windows. Jennifer pointed. "I can only imagine the show you put on for your neighbors."

Brooke bumped her hip with her own. "Amusing." She paused for a minute and then continued. "We always try to remember to pull the shades." She shot Jennifer a playful smile. "Let's grab a beer and go sit out back. It's so nice today."

Jennifer followed Brooke out to the kitchen where they took bottles out of the fridge and an extra two for Tyler and Caden.

She opened the sliding glass door, and Tyler smiled at Brooke with the extra bottles in her hands. "You're amazing."

Brooke handed out the extra beers. "Don't forget that." Brooke kissed Tyler on the forehead.

Jennifer took a seat next to Caden and opened her bottle. "Agent Styles."

Caden lifted her drink toward her. "Always lovely to see you, Analyst Glass."

Tyler raised her eyebrows and turned her attention toward Brooke. "What time is Patrick coming over?"

Brooke glanced down at her watch. "Should be here any minute."

Tyler nodded. "I invited Nicole and Kyle, but they're in the middle of testing out a class."

Brooke smiled at Jennifer. "The good ole days."

Jennifer huffed. "I don't know how good they were."

Caden, who could never seem to help herself, interjected. "I can't imagine anything more pleasant than being locked in a facility for a year or two with you and your cheery disposition, Jen."

Jennifer shot her a sideways glance and rolled her eyes.

"Hello?" Patrick's voice drifted out the screen door over the music. Brooke leaped up from her seat and ran inside to meet Patrick. There were very few people on the planet she loved more than Patrick Bowing. Patrick wrapped her in a giant hug, picking her up off the ground and swinging her around.

Caden watched the exchange and then looked at Tyler. "Does that ever bother you?"

Tyler was smiling, watching Brooke and Patrick. "What? Those two?"

Caden nodded and Tyler continued. "No. They're best friends. And in case you haven't noticed, *he* isn't her type." Tyler went inside.

Jennifer looked over at Caden. "Not everyone is insecure and self-centered."

Caden leaned closer to her. "And not everyone knows a good thing when it's standing in front of them."

Jennifer leaned even closer, anger starting to consume her. "What exactly are you implying, Caden?"

The door reopened, and Tyler came out with a plate of food in her hand. Brooke and Patrick followed a few steps behind, laughing. Caden sat back, her grin daring Jennifer to keep talking. Jennifer sat back and plastered a smile on her face. No way she'd be the one to start drama among the group. Not today, anyway.

❖

Tyler and Caden were standing at the BBQ discussing something that required Tyler to use a lot of animated hand signals. Brooke leaned her head back and watched. Contentment filled her chest, and a smile escaped her lips.

Jennifer nudged her. "Were you even listening to us?"

Brooke looked at Jen and Patrick. "What happened?"

Patrick chuckled. "You know, you're just as mesmerized with her as you were the day she strolled into our classroom."

Brooke shook her head. "That's not true."

Jennifer added. "Oh no, it's way worse now."

Brooke didn't argue; she just continued to smile. Brooke was etching this moment into her memory for a later time. The feel of the dwindling sun seemed to be lightly kissing her cheeks, the laughter of her friends, and the closeness of Tyler, warmed her chest. Everything was perfect.

Brooke looked at Jennifer thoughtfully before she continued. "What about you, Jen? Meet any special men lately?"

Jen glared at her. "Ha! Do you think I met someone in the week since I last saw you?"

She said it playfully, but there was no emotion in her voice. Brooke followed her line of site. It was on Caden. Jennifer had previously mentioned how impressed she was with Caden's physicality. Brooke had thought nothing of it at the time. She had assumed it was just a straight woman appreciating the appearance of another woman. But watching Jen's eyes now, she saw it. It wasn't appreciation; it was lust. Brooke looked at Caden, trying to see her through Jen's eyes. Caden's solid arms were accented by her tight blue, sheer tank top. Her faded blue jeans and large belt buckle captured only the front of the almost see-through shirt, hinting at the shell of her defined, "Made by Homeland Security," stomach. Her ink-black hair was pulled back in a loose ponytail, showing off her seemingly perfect bone structure. *Yeah, okay. I can see it.*

Jen finally pulled her eyes away. "Nope, no men."

Brooke wasn't going to call her out. Not here and not now.

Patrick, on the other hand, seemed oblivious and offered his insight. "Obviously, you haven't met any men because I'm your benchmark. Who could compete with that?" He laughed, earning him a smile and a smack from Jennifer.

"You, Patrick Bowing, might be spending entirely too much time over in Homeland Security. I think Styles might have slipped you a bit of whatever confidence serum she injects every morning."

Brooke absorbed the easy banter and familiar laughter. It filled her senses and consumed her awareness. She felt as if she belonged here, not just in this moment, but with these people. There was no communal blood between them, they didn't share a family tree or any type of lineage, but they were family all the same. Brooke felt a twinge of melancholy at the back of her throat, and felt a little sad she had never shared this with any of her siblings or parents, or even cousins for that matter. She pushed the twinge away, deciding to be grateful for the moment all the same. *Grateful.* Yes, that was the perfect word for it.

CHAPTER THREE

The temperature had shifted drastically, dropping at least thirty degrees from the warmth of the day. The heat coming from the fire pit and the consistent crackling from the logs was soothing. Tyler's phone rang, disrupting the peaceful moment. She excused herself into the apartment to take the call. Jennifer watched Brooke as Brooke watched Tyler. She wondered for maybe the millionth time what it would be like to be so in tune with another person, so devoted. Jennifer had long ago decided that Brooke and Tyler were an anomaly. They had something not everyone was gifted with in a lifetime. She didn't realize she'd started staring at Caden as she went through her internal reflection. Caden glanced over at her for a moment, just a passing second. It seemed as though she might know what Jennifer was thinking, but she turned her attention away as her phone started vibrating.

Jennifer watched the lines in Caden's face change. Moments before, her eyes had been warm and inviting. Now, though, she was clearly on alert. Not worried; there was no fear buried in the lines between her eyes. Rather, it was intense awareness. These transitions in her expressions were something Jennifer had memorized over time. The way Caden's eyes smiled first and then her mouth followed. The way she wore all her intensity in her brow and how her jaw would clench intermittently. They were little things, predictable things, a handful of things Jennifer had collected over time and kept tucked away. She held on to them like little treasures, evidence of how well she knew Caden. Proof to herself that it was real, that it had been real, even if only for a moment.

Caden, who always seemed to know when Jen was looking at her, glanced back at her. She tried to smile, but this one didn't reach her eyes. Jennifer knew what the call was. They all did. It was something they had been waiting for, anticipating, and preparations had been made. Jennifer knew where Caden would end up tonight. It was the same place she always ended up a few hours after one of those calls. She would be placing herself in danger, and Jennifer had no right to tell her about the panic she felt welling in her chest. The tingling sensation of anxiety she felt every time Caden strapped on her vest and walked out the door always made her slightly dizzy. She had forfeited that right a long time ago, and there was nothing she could do to get it back, even if it were what she wanted.

❖

Brooke, responding to Tyler's wave, went inside. She shut the sliding glass door and turned around to face Tyler.

"I wanted to talk to you about this sooner, but I was waiting until I had some definitive information."

Brooke nodded.

"We found Lark."

Tyler should've been surprised at Brooke's insight, but she wasn't. Tyler put her hands on Brooke's shoulders. "Caden and I have to go. Tonight."

Brooke wanted to protest. She hated the idea of Tyler going into some dark, undisclosed location and putting herself in danger for the likes of a madman. Brooke wanted to see Lark pay. She wanted him to face terrorism charges, wanted him buried in some hole that only a few people knew about, to live out the remainder of his days alone and depleted. Tyler and Caden were the perfect people to get it done. It *was* personal, and Tyler needed her support, not her fear. "Caden is going with you?"

Tyler nodded. "Caden and six other people."

Brooke grabbed the sides of Tyler's face and kissed her. Brooke wasn't able to find the words she needed to say, and she hoped the kiss could convey her thoughts and feelings. The need for Tyler to return safely and unscarred vibrated through her veins, pumped with each beat of her heart, as involuntary and necessary as breathing. Brooke needed Tyler to come back to her; there was no other option.

Caden came in, finishing with her phone call. "You ready?"

Tyler hugged Brooke and kissed her forehead, promising her return. She nodded once at Caden, and Brooke watched as Tyler's face changed. Moments before, Tyler had been her loving partner, but now she was all soldier. Even her eye color seemed to shift, becoming more like ice. It was the only comparison Brooke had. They were out the front door and gone before another word was said.

Brooke stormed back out into the yard. Both Patrick's and Jen's eyes were on her, and she realized that neither knew what to say. Brooke broke the silence. "Well, don't just sit there. Let's get down to Langley."

Jennifer shifted in her seat. She gave Brooke the sense that she was uncomfortable with the request. "We can't."

Brooke put her hands on her hips and stared at her. "What do you mean? This is your assignment, isn't it?"

Jennifer shrugged. "It's out of my hands. My assignment was to help locate the target. I have nothing to do with it now."

Brooke started pacing. Various emotions flooded through her, but the one she honed in on was her annoyance. "How long have you known where he was?"

Jennifer slumped down in her seat. "Not long."

Brooke knew her anger at Jennifer was irrational, but she couldn't seem to help herself. "You should've warned me!"

Jennifer shook her head. "You know I can't do that, Brooke. There was a reason I was assigned to this case and you weren't. Look at you!"

Brooke's immediate response was to be angry, but Jennifer was right. She was acting ridiculous. She flopped down in her seat, staring at Jennifer and Patrick. "I know. You're right. I just feel so damn useless sitting here doing nothing."

Jennifer moved a few seats over and took Brooke's hand before she spoke. "Tyler and Caden are the very best at what they do, and they're going to take care of this asshole and then we can all finally move on."

Brooke squeezed her fingers, grateful for the compassion in Jen's eyes. "You're right, thank you."

"What do you need us to do?" Patrick asked.

Brooke looked at them and then finally answered. "I need to hit something."

Jennifer closed her eyes. "Why do I have a feeling we're going to be spending the next several hours in a gym?"

Brooke patted her hand and got up. "Because you're an excellent analyst and an even better friend."

Jennifer looked over at Patrick, who shrugged and got up. "I'll drive."

Brooke reached for the passenger door but then stopped. It felt as if someone was watching her. *Nerves. Don't let this guy get in your head.* She looked up and down the street, and although everything seemed normal, and there was nothing obviously suspicious, she couldn't shake the feeling. She turned her attention to the apartment building across the street, which was under construction.

Jennifer stood with the door open and looked at her over the roof of the car. "What's wrong?"

Brooke was staring up at one of the windows, sure she had just seen something move inside. "I just feel like we're being watched."

Jennifer tapped the roof of the car. "We all feel like that, and it won't stop until Lark is in custody."

Brooke pulled her gaze away from the building and looked at Jennifer. "Right. You're right." She pulled open the door and got in. "Let's go."

Brooke knew that Jen was probably right. They were all on edge and had been for as long as she could remember. It was probably her mind playing tricks on her, or it could have been someone up in that building with a perfectly good explanation. They drove past the building, and she looked up at it one more time. *Nerves. Just nerves.*

CHAPTER FOUR

The driver made the announcement to the van. "ETA fifteen minutes."

Tyler glanced at the communications van following to make sure they were keeping up, and then looked at the six men in the vehicle with her. Each was checking his weapon and adjusting his equipment. The team was ready and focused. She could almost taste the adrenaline in the air.

Caden adjusted her gloves and looked up at Tyler. "How many lives do you have left, little cat?"

It was a nickname Caden had bestowed upon Tyler during one of their many training sessions. Tyler's ability to sneak up on her target was like nothing Caden had ever seen. Tyler grinned. "Seven."

Caden grunted her disbelief before Tyler continued.

"But I'm on my fourth cat." They smiled at each other, and Tyler was incredibly glad it was Caden at her back for this one.

Both vans came to an eerily quiet stop. All eight team members filed out and lined up, waiting for the signal to proceed. There was no need to go over the plan again. Their training was as ingrained in their brains as breathing. Caden went to the right and Tyler to the left, three men following in each of their wakes. The night air was damp and heavy, and the smells of the earth filled Tyler's senses as she made her way toward the entrance of the compound. Tyler hesitated. It was too quiet. They'd been planning this maneuver for two weeks, ever since they'd found Lark, but the decision to go on this particular evening had only been made two hours prior, when she'd received the phone call. Either they were expecting their arrival, which seemed unlikely, or they'd already moved on. *Something's not right. What the hell is going on?* She'd always preferred the enemy to be lying in wait rather than allowed to escape.

Tyler pushed the radio link button at her neck. "Snipers, take your position."

"Roger." The voice crackled in her earpiece.

One of the men trailing her disappeared up onto a rock fifty feet away, and she knew one of Caden's men was doing the same. Tyler flipped on her infrared goggles and took twenty quiet paces to the fence line. She quickly glanced around the corner and scanned the facility. No red imagery took shape. She gave a forward signal to the man directly behind her, and he grabbed a small silver orb out of his cargo pants and rolled it into the entrance. He held a small piece up to his ear and then shook his head. The sphere was designed to scan a five-hundred-foot radius for electrical pings. A ping would indicate a bomb in the designated boundary.

She pushed her radio link again. "Status check."

Caden's voice came on at once. "No targets located. Proceeding."

The fence line briefly shook, and the metallic rustle penetrated Tyler's senses as she mentally calculated the distance between herself and the muffled noise. She took the corner, the two men following closely behind. She fixed on a lump curled next to the fence. As she closed the distance, it was evident the lump wasn't going to move forward or attack. Its arms were up in a position of surrender. As Tyler got closer, she could hear the figure crying, whimpering with fear. She flipped up her goggles and lowered her weapon while the men behind her kept their guns trained on the unknown target.

"Please don't hurt me."

The voice was shaking, but the tone was wrong. There was a vulnerability missing, and Tyler watched carefully. She grabbed her flashlight and aimed it at the woman's chest, not wanting to ignite fear by blinding her, but enough to illuminate her face and to scan for visible weapons.

"What's your name?" Tyler's question held no room for argument. Their target was missing, and instead there was a woman lying right in their path. She hated when things weren't going as planned.

"Rowen, Rowen Knight." The woman had tears streaking down her cheeks, creating a clear trail in the dirt smudged all over her face. "They've been holding me here for days, possibly even weeks." She looked around before she continued. "Then about two hours ago, everyone just disappeared. I waited because I was scared they'd be back and they'd catch me if I ran, but no one ever came."

Tyler motioned for the men to lower their weapons as she gently took the woman's arm, pulling her to her feet. Tyler scanned her up and down. "Why aren't you restrained?"

The woman looked back into the compound before she continued, as though waiting for them to come rushing out. "They had me in a flimsy wooden cell. I was able to kick it open once there was no longer a guard standing over me constantly."

Tyler wasn't convinced. There was something off about her story, but she was willing to play along for now. "We're going to take you into custody, get you situated. Hopefully, you can help us fill in some of the blanks about what has been going on here."

"Who are you?" Rowan asked, sniffling.

Tyler didn't want to give her an outright answer until she knew more. "We're part of the government, ma'am. We're going to help you."

❖

Brooke hit the heavy bag for what must have been the five thousandth time. The chain that secured the bag to the ceiling beam rattled with force. Sweat rolled down her shoulders and exposed stomach. The events of the past year jumped from her psyche with each grunt. Brooke remembered vividly what it had felt like to sit over her partner's bloody body after one of Lark's henchman, Thompson, had attempted to kill her. Memories of Tyler's cold hands and glazed eyes sliced through her heart. The fear that had gripped her that night was still haunting her, almost mocking her from a corner of her mind that she could never fully banish.

Lark's penetration into the secrets of the CIA had been unfathomable. Thompson had managed to infiltrate the Farm and had almost gained access to Top Secret CIA files that would've not only unmasked nearly every operative in circulation, but all their known associates and acquaintances as well. They also would've gotten their hands on every emergency evacuation procedure for the executive branch. The devastation he wanted to unleash would've been like nothing the United States had ever seen. Lark was meticulous, smart, wealthy, and even worse, patient. He'd taken his own son, Agent Chris Carlson, and molded him into a terrorist who had spent his whole life with one mission in mind. Carlson joined the CIA with the sole intent of taking it down. If it hadn't been for Thompson's hatred of Tyler, they might have succeeded.

Brooke dropped to her knees, trying to catch her breath. Sweat started to sting her eyes. She pulled off her gloves and accepted the towel Jennifer tossed her from a folding chair she was sitting on ten feet away. "Why can't we be like normal friends and just go drink our troubles away?"

The comment earned Jennifer a smile. "Normal is overrated." Brooke looked around the gym. "Where is Patrick?"

Jennifer pointed to a bench over in the corner of the large workout area where Patrick was curled up, sleeping. Brooke looked down at her watch. "I didn't realize I had been at this for so long."

Jennifer sat next to her on the mat. "You were in a zone. It happens." She paused briefly. "It never happens to me, but it apparently happens."

Brooke accepted her attempt to lighten her mood. "I'm going to go take a shower and then we can get out of here." Brooke stood up. "Thanks for being here. I really didn't want to be alone."

Jennifer nodded. "Anytime. Besides, I think I owe you a few after how horrible I was to you while we were at the Farm."

Brooke was surprised by the statement. She hadn't realized Jennifer still felt guilty about that. "Where did that come from?"

Jennifer shrugged. "It's hard not to think about those times when we're right on the brink of catching Lark."

Brooke picked up her water bottle and desperately gulped down the liquid inside. She enjoyed the way the cool fluid seemed to rush through her limbs, offering a bit of relief to her tired body.

"I was insanely jealous of you, you know," Jennifer said.

Brooke had never considered why Jennifer was so cold to her during their training days. She'd always just assumed that Jennifer was a guarded person, which made it difficult for people to get to know her, but once training was over and they'd gotten to know one another, she'd mellowed out. "Jealous of me? Why?"

Jennifer's posture slumped slightly. "That right there. You should be overconfident, arrogant, but you aren't. Everything seems to come so easily to you. It's always seemed so effortless, and I really hate that about you." Jennifer stood and looked at Brooke. Her blue eyes were full of emotion. "I finally realized it would be easier to be kind to you than to continue to hate you for being perfect."

Brooke rolled her eyes. "I'm far from perfect."

Jennifer seemed to suppress a laugh. "I wish that were true, Hart."

Brooke ran the towel over herself, trying to soak up some of the moisture her body insisted on continuing to dump. "I'm insecure at times, I get angry easily, I'm impatient, and I really don't like change. And those are just off the top of my head. I'm sure Tyler could give you a much more detailed list."

Jennifer pushed Brooke toward the locker room to shower. "I seriously doubt that."

A dozen minutes later, Brooke left the locker room to meet her two friends, who were waiting for her with anxious looks on their faces. "What's wrong?" Brooke's heart had quickly jumped from her stomach to her throat based solely on their expressions. *Please don't let it be Tyler. Not again.*

"They're on their way back and they have a prisoner." Jennifer gripped Brooke's shoulder. "Check your phone."

Brooke pulled the device out of the side pocket of her bag and checked the text messages. *Report to Interrogation Sector B.*

Patrick hugged Brooke and then started toward the front door. "I need to shower and then head to a briefing. Call me and fill me in on what you can later?"

He was asking the question as the door swung open. Brooke barely managed a reply before the door closed. "Sure."

Brooke and Jennifer turned back toward the locker room. They needed to change into clothes more fitting of CIA agents instead of gym rats. "What are you thinking?" Jennifer asked.

"I think it isn't Lark that they have in custody, or they wouldn't need me."

"I thought the same thing," Jennifer said.

Brooke's relief was fleeting. Tyler was alive and apparently in one piece, but a prisoner could mean a number of things, none of which were good. Lark wasn't sloppy. He didn't leave loose ends, and that's exactly what this prisoner was, a loose end.

CHAPTER FIVE

Where're we going?"

Tyler looked at Rowen, taking a moment to study her a little more carefully. She was average height but muscular. She knew her firm arms and legs weren't forged in the gym through power training because they were lean and toned, much like her own. Her arms and neck were covered in dirt and grime, but there were no noticeable scrapes or bruises, something you would assume would be prevalent after a week or so of being held hostage. Her hair was a vibrant red. It reminded Tyler of a sunset, or perhaps the fire from hell, depending on how this turned out. Her eyes were green like Brooke's, but there was no comparison. Rowen's eyes seemed dull and emotionless. "Somewhere safe." Tyler answered, still unwilling to give any more information than necessary. She'd feel bad later if Rowen was genuinely a victim, but her intuition told her there were things going on she couldn't see yet.

Tyler shifted her gaze to Caden, who met her eyes. Caden tilted her head slightly, as though asking a question. She seemed confused, and Tyler assumed it was because of the way she was reacting to Rowen. She'd normally never treat a possible victim with such gruff distance. Tyler was being purposely obtuse, and Caden knew her well enough to know that it was for a good reason.

Cynicism in these situations ran deep in Tyler. She had learned the hard way in Iraq that people aren't always what they seem. She had lost men on two different occasions in situations that seemed eerily familiar to this. The first time, they'd approached a child on the side of the road because he appeared to need help, only to be lured slightly off course and ambushed. The second time, a woman crying for help had an M16 hidden under her abaya.

Tyler knew it wasn't true for all the people she encountered there. Most were good, honest people that wanted what everyone else wanted—for their children to have a better life than they did and for peace in their country. The radicals made that impossible with their mission of death and destruction. They would murder and endanger their own people to advance their agenda, with no regard for the body count they left in their wake. The Taliban would sacrifice anything and anyone to make their voices heard.

The realization that some people could kill without discretion and without regard to consequence because they believed their cause was more significant than anyone else, lived inside Tyler. It wasn't something she could unlearn. The knowledge that people were capable of heinous, bloody, brutal acts when they believed they were for the right reasons would be with her for the rest of her life. Propaganda, rhetoric, brainwashing, call it whatever you want, those were the ingredients of the nightmares that haunted her.

Tyler wasn't sure who this woman was, what she wanted, or if she could be trusted. It didn't matter; she was going to err on the side of caution until those questions could be answered. Despite what people believed, Al-Qaeda, ISIL, and Al-Nusra didn't have the market cornered on terrorism. Anger and hatred live everywhere, and just like any poison, those attributes could be easily turned in to a deadly cocktail, ready to be unleashed on the holder's choosing. When Tyler looked at Rowen, she didn't see a victim. She'd seen more than enough of them to know what they looked like—the haunted look in their eyes, the fear, the anguish. The woman in the room didn't have any of those hallmarks. Tyler knew a predator when she saw one.

❖

Brooke silently wondered why clandestine agencies insisted on using all-black, unmarked vehicles for every operation she'd ever taken part in or studied. In her opinion, the fact that they were so unbelievably plain was what made them conspicuous. She pushed the thought away as she watched the van that held Tyler, Caden, and a third party pull into the underground parking structure. Brooke turned away from the closed-circuit monitoring system and faced her bank of computers. She began launching a variety of programs, from facial recognition software to the INTERPOL database. Another analyst set a cup of coffee next to Brooke's workstation when the double doors flung open, and a low, rumbling voice filled the room.

"This better be good."

Brooke closed her eyes to stop her eye roll. Ryan Rezentes, technical analyst manager, Brooke's boss and all around tool, could never just enter a room without making his presence, and disdain, known. Rezentes was probably in his early forties but looked in his late fifties, thanks to his rapidly disappearing hairline, bulging gut, and cranky attitude. He held a strong set of outdated and disgusting opinions regarding politics, women in the CIA, and the gay community as a whole. He was one of the few people in the world that could make Brooke's blood boil by merely existing. He was rarely on site for anything but had decided to make an appearance here and now. Brooke blew out a long breath and tried to gather herself. *Don't let him get to you. Calm and collected. Breathe.* She inhaled, and his distinct odor assaulted her, the scent of stale cigarettes and a cheap aftershave clouding the air next to her as he stared at her screen.

"Anything yet?"

Brooke bit back her retort; of course, there was nothing yet. They were just in the process of entering the building. "No, sir, we're waiting for Agents Styles and Monroe from Homeland Security to bring the prisoner into the holding room."

He grumbled, saying something Brooke couldn't make out. She glanced to her left where he stood. Her eyes were level with his belly, and she saw the buttons on his shirt struggling to hold the material together as it moved in and out, matching his labored breathing. It wasn't the first time Brooke wondered how he had ascended into this position of authority. Ryan Rezentes was a stark contrast to other supervisors Brooke had encountered during her time with the CIA. He lacked empathy for those around him and those affected by him, and he seemed to only care about himself. From everything Brooke could tell, he wasn't a good person, and she instinctually didn't trust him. Being in this close proximity to his body made her shudder.

Jennifer took the seat next to her and started to pull up the satellite imagery from the compound Homeland Security was still in the process of securing. She began listing some notable markers, and it managed to draw Rezentes's attention away. Brooke silently thanked her, making a note to buy her a drink next time they were out together.

Brooke watched the screens as Tyler walked down the hallway, a woman between her and Caden. Brooke stared intently at the monitors. Tyler wasn't limping, didn't seem to be hurt, and didn't even appear to be dirty. The crushing weight that was always present when Tyler went out on assignment disappeared in that instant. Tyler stopped in front of a large metal door and turned around to look at Rowen. Tyler was watching Rowan's hands, which she'd secured in a set of zip ties. Brooke knew that Tyler had purposely tied her hands in front of her and not behind her to build a sense of trust. She understood this meant Tyler must think there was information she could garner from her detainee.

Well, at least that's something. She watched as Tyler maneuvered the woman so her face was toward the camera, and she saw the faintest smirk appear on the woman's face. *She knows we're running facial recognition.* A chill went up Brooke's back. Tyler was right to keep the woman in cuffs. Something wasn't right.

❖

Caden watched Rowen's reaction as they brought her into the room. She seemed to appraise the accommodations quickly. The room had a small, neutral brown couch, a kitchenette, and an enclosed bathroom.

Rowen glanced at the ceiling, clearly noting the cameras in each of the corners. "What a fancy prison cell you've brought me to, Agent."

Tyler's face showed no expression as she spoke. "It's intended to keep you safe until we figure out what's going on. It isn't a prison cell."

Rowen held out her hands to Caden so she could cut the ties off, her stare intense and probing. She felt like Rowen was searching for something.

"Isn't it, though?"

Caden methodically cut off the white zip ties from Rowen's wrists. Tyler pulled out one of the chairs and sat down, and Caden leaned against the wall while Rowen took a seat on the couch.

Tyler stared at Rowen intently. "Are you thirsty?"

Rowen nodded, and Tyler got up to retrieve a cup from the small cupboard.

As she let the tap water run into the glass, she spoke. "There'll be a medic by in a few minutes to check you out. I don't want to overwhelm you, so after that, you can get some rest and we can talk again in the morning."

Rowen's back went rigid at the statement. "You intend to keep me here overnight?"

Tyler cocked a half smile in her direction and wrapped her words in what Caden knew was obvious sarcasm. "I don't want you in any danger. Those people who captured you are still out there, and we don't want anything to happen to you."

Caden interjected. "Is there anyone we need to call for you? Is there someone we should notify about your safety?"

Rowen turned her attention to her now. Caden watched Rowen's eyes travel up and down her body. Caden had seen the look before, though never from a suspect in custody. It was a look of appreciation and seduction. "No. There's no one."

A muted beep came from the door right before it swung open, and two medics came through. Tyler motioned to Caden. "Let's give her some privacy." Caden pushed herself off the wall with a single movement and followed Tyler.

Caden's head was spinning, unable to make sense of what just happened. If Rowen was truly a hostage, she would be scared, nervous, and probably suffering from PTSD. This wasn't the case at all. Her behavior, actions, and even her words were a melting pot of mixed signals. In one moment, she played the role of being scared and unsure of what was happening. In the next, she was confident, powerful, and giving off a hyper-sexual vibe. Caden wasn't sure what that meant, but she knew it wasn't good.

They walked through the stark hallways, heading toward the monitoring facility. There were several moments before Tyler spoke. "Thoughts?"

"Still too early to say, but she isn't giving us the whole story."

Tyler pushed the last doorway open. "My thoughts exactly."

They reached the monitoring facility several minutes later and pushed the button for access. The door buzzed, and Tyler and Caden entered the controlled chaos of monitors and whirring computers. Ryan Rezentes turned, made brief eye contact, and then turned his attention back toward the monitors. "What the fuck do you two want?"

Tyler's body flinched, but before she could respond to him with the same venom in her voice, Caden cut her off, knowing full well a confrontation between the two would only land Tyler in hot water.

"Just checking in before we head back to DHS." Caden smirked at Tyler. She purposely used the acronym DHS instead of Department of Homeland Security because it pissed Rezentes off. She'd heard it was because he thought it was their way of equating themselves to the CIA. It didn't help matters that they were the lead agents for the Office of Intelligence and Analysis, which was another redundant department in Rezentes's mind. He scowled at them, obviously searching his brain for a dickish response, but Caden cut him off again. "You know, Rezentes, whenever you want to come over to DHS and use our gym, you're always welcome."

Rezentes straightened as though trying to suck in his gut. "We have a state-of-the-art training facility right here."

Caden tried to look incredulous and looked him over. "You're kidding? You might want to check that out."

Jennifer had turned her chair around, presumably to take in the interaction. The smile that crept across her face at Caden's remarks was subtle but undeniable. Caden enjoyed making her smile, even if it was fleeting.

He turned his attention to them, clearly on the verge of launching into a full on verbal attack, when Brooke spoke up.

"INTERPOL came back without any hits, but we have had a few pings on the intelligence server. I need to put in a request for access, but we won't get that for a few hours."

Tyler responded, blatantly ignoring Rezentes. "Keep us updated."

Brooke half turned her chair and smiled. "Roger that, Special Agent Monroe."

Caden managed a single wink in Rezentes's direction and they left in the midst of his huffing and puffing.

Once outside the double doors, Tyler glanced over at Caden, who felt the arrogance radiating off her. She couldn't help it; he brought out every ounce of it she had in her. Her thumbs were tucked into her belt loops, and her cheeks hurt from smiling so widely. Caden let out a deep sigh before she spoke. "He just makes it so damn easy."

Tyler blew out a long breath. "He is an obnoxious bastard, isn't he?"

Caden grabbed Tyler's shoulder as they got into their van. "Tyler Monroe. Did you just say something bad about someone?" She paused so she could truly feign surprise. "Without them here to defend themselves?"

Tyler pulled open the back door to the van and climbed in. "That's nothing, Styles. You should hear what I say about you."

Caden cocked her head and squinted at Tyler, who was obviously fighting back a smile. Caden adjusted her equipment as she spoke. "If it weren't for my love of Brooke, I'd kick your ass right here." Caden settled back into her seat, glad she'd never have to put that theory to the test. The van made the final check to leave the CIA facility and started maneuvering down the long drive. Caden wasn't a fan of silence, and it bugged her that Tyler seemed far away. "No witty retorts, Monroe?"

Tyler shook her head like she was waking herself from a daydream. "I'm sorry. What was that? I was trying to count all the times I have already kicked your ass."

Caden smiled. "There she is."

❖

Caden and Tyler replaced their gear in the equipment storage locker. They were checking in their vests when a young man came bursting through the doors.

"He wants to see you right away." The young man looked frantic. He was clearly a newbie, and this was probably his first substantial assignment. His head was likely swimming with protocol and policies.

Tyler and Caden walked up next to him and Caden motioned in the direction of the main corridor. "After you, Sparky."

Tyler rolled her eyes. "Ignore her. She always thinks she's funnier than she is after an assignment. The adrenaline messes with her head."

He didn't seem to notice Caden's comment or Tyler's explanation. He was hurrying through the hallways, leading them to a briefing room they'd both been in a few dozen times. He pushed the doors open, stood there for a minute, and then, as if a light bulb went on in his head, he said, "Water. I'll grab you both some water."

Caden and Tyler went to sit down. The kid didn't require an answer, he was on autopilot at this point, and he disappeared down the hall. They'd both been there before, and Tyler felt older than her years as she watched him go.

Moments later, Jared Martin entered the room. Four other suits followed in right after and all took their seats around the table. Jared Martin's official title was Deputy Director of the Office of Intelligence and Analysis. Tyler both respected and liked him. He was fair, concise, smart, and had a sense of humor. The Marine Corps hadn't afforded her a tremendous amount of opportunities to work for someone with all those attributes, and she enjoyed taking his direction and learning from him. Jared leaned forward and put his hands on the table, which made him seem more accessible. Tyler wasn't sure if it was intentional or just inherent in his nature, it didn't matter. The motion did help to put her at ease.

"Before we start, let me say that you and your team did an outstanding job."

Tyler shifted a bit in her seat as she sensed there was a "but" coming.

Director Martin continued. "We now have someone in custody I think will be able to give us some insight into Lark and his cronies. Intel that brings us that much closer to catching him, once and for all."

Tyler wanted to interject. She made eye contact with the deputy director, something she would've never done in the Marine Corps.

He noticed. "Thoughts?"

Tyler considered before she spoke, a habit she'd always had. Many people interpreted the brief silence as her dismissal of a conversation or her not having anything to add, but Martin seemed to understand the way she worked, and he waited patiently. "Sir, I don't believe Rowen Knight is who she says she is. I don't trust her. It feels like she's playing a game of some kind."

One of the faceless suits from the other side of the table interrupted. "A game?" He clearly wasn't convinced, and there was a mocking tone in his voice. "Special Agent, you'd have us believe this woman made up her entire story?"

Tyler glanced in his direction, not bothering to really look at him. She wasn't judging him, she wasn't arguing, she was just stating a fact. "Yes."

The man let out a mild laugh. "Based on what, Special Agent?"

Tyler's response was instant. "A gut feeling."

The man scoffed in disbelief. Another suit who sat next to him decided to add his two cents. "So you suggest what... we treat her like a prisoner? A woman you found lying on the ground, who said she'd been a captive?"

Tyler looked at them both thoughtfully as she continued. "I don't expect you two will be doing much of anything." She turned her attention back to Deputy Director Jared Martin. "I suggest we give the CIA time. Time to find out if she is who she says she is. They already had a hit when we left, and they were just waiting on approval to retrieve the information." Tyler looked at everyone seated around the table. "And even when we do find out, I think we should keep it to ourselves until we have the opportunity to see the tale she spins."

Deputy Director Martin looked around the table. "Get out." It was stated with simplicity, totally void of emotion. The men looked at each other briefly, probably trying to decipher his meaning. He nodded toward the door behind him. "Get out."

Tyler fought back her smile. No one dared say a word. The men pushed their chairs back and filed out of the room. The door closed behind the last starched gray suit.

Martin tapped his fingers on the tabletop, thinking. Finally, he said, "It could be a media nightmare. Keeping someone locked up for questioning that had already been held captive for weeks. People are all over this kind of thing nowadays. The government and its tactics are always on trial in the court of public opinion. Usually, we could keep this under wraps, but there was a traffic chopper in the sky that caught a glimpse of your team taking the compound. Hence, the four jokers that came with me. All public relations and lawyers."

"I don't think anyone could blame us for wanting to check her story out. No one knows we have her. She told me herself there wasn't anyone we needed to call. We don't have to say she's a prisoner, or even a person of interest. We can say she's here for her own protection. Which could turn out to be true," Caden added.

The deputy director nodded. "It's settled then. You two continue to run point on this. Work with the CIA. I want a daily briefing on the progress."

Martin had just left the room when Tyler's phone buzzed. It was a text message from Brooke.

Not going to be home for a while. Get some sleep. Love you.

Tyler started toward the door. "Come on. Let's get out of here." Caden hesitated for a moment. Tyler put her hand on her hip. "What's the problem, Styles?"

Caden made her way over to where Tyler was standing. She reached into her pocket and handed Tyler the keys. "Drive yourself home. Just bring the car back when you come back. I'm going to monitor the prisoner situation."

Tyler bounced the keys around in her hand as she studied Caden. She decided not to ask more. She wasn't entirely sure what was going through Caden's head, but if Caden wanted her to know, she would've said something. Tyler wasn't one to pry into people's innermost thoughts, and she respected people's need to work things out on their own before talking them through, if that's what they needed to do. Tyler glanced down at her watch. "Okay. I'll see you in a few hours."

"Yeah, you got it." Caden said as she left.

Tyler wasn't entirely sure what Caden was up to, but she trusted her. If Caden was on to something she would let her know. Kinks or splinters in their trust could fracture more than their friendship; it could weaken their partnership. They needed to know and believe they had each other's backs. Their lives depended on it.

❖

Tyler's mind was still moving in about a million different directions when she turned down her street. *My street.* The thought was still so foreign. Tyler hadn't called any place home since she was a teenager. The shabbily assembled camps she'd utilized in the Marine Corps were all Tyler thought she'd ever know. She smiled as a feeling of happiness and home wrapped around her. *That's Brooke. She's my home.*

Her thoughts were cut off mid-process by an unfamiliar vehicle parked on the street. Tyler hadn't meant to memorize the usual cars that occupied this area; it was just habit. She could see the emblem on the back bumper, identifying itself as a rental car. A quick inspection as she drove by showed that the car was empty, with both seats in their upright position. *Okay, no one lying in wait.* She parked Caden's car on the street and went around to the trunk. Tyler grabbed her 9mm from the holster and started toward the apartment. She peered through the slotted, wrought iron gates to get a glimpse of the backside of the apartment. She didn't see any movement, but that did little to squelch the foreboding in her stomach. Tyler glanced down at her watch; it was almost eight in the morning. She couldn't imagine who would have the nerve to be rifling through someone's apartment at this hour. She forced herself to slow down and think it through. It wouldn't be a clandestine operative. They'd be much more careful; they would've never left a rental car in plain view on the street. Slowly, she made her way to her front door and opened the handle. She could make out voices in the bedroom, but she couldn't be sure how many people there were. She slid across the entryway, gun at the ready. She heard the footsteps coming closer. She knelt, knowing she could take a shot from this position with little risk to her own safety.

The voices were unfamiliar. "I don't know what time she'll be home, Calvin. Apparently, we aren't important enough to leave work for."

Tyler felt her heart thumping at the back of her throat. There really wasn't anything that scared her, intimidated her, or made her life flash before her eyes. Except, that is, for Brooke's parents, who happened to be five feet away. Tyler stood just as they came around the corner.

Janice Hart looked Tyler up and down slowly as her perfectly manicured fingernails covered her heart. Her mouth formed a frown that Tyler had seen at least a hundred times before on Brooke's face. Janice was clearly not impressed with the disheveled mess standing in front of her. Tyler became very aware of how she must look. She transferred her gun to her other hand and tried to hold it slightly behind her.

She tried to speak, but Janice cut her off.

"You must be the roommate. Tyler isn't it?"

Tyler shook off the comment. Janice knew exactly who she was to Brooke, and it wasn't her problem if Brooke's mom couldn't handle it. Tyler put her hand out. "Nice to meet you."

Janice didn't reach for her hand, but Captain Calvin Hart, Brooke's father, took it as he spoke. "We're sorry to drop in on you like this. We were in town for a small consulting job that I'm doing and figured we'd stop by." Tyler nodded and he continued, sounding genuinely apologetic. "We called Brooke and she called maintenance to let us in."

Janice was eyeing the gun in Tyler's hand, which suddenly seemed to weigh a thousand pounds.

She pointed. "Do you always come to my daughter's home with your weapon drawn?"

Tyler closed her eyes, silently cursing Brooke for not getting a hold of her to warn her about this visit. *Christ, babe. I know you're busy, but geez.* She moved past them and into the kitchen, unloading the gun as she walked. "No. I'm sorry. I normally wouldn't. I didn't know you'd be here, and I'm not used to coming home and having people in my apartment." She opened the small handgun safe in their kitchen and placed the weapon inside.

Janice let out an annoyed sigh. "How many of those do you have?"

Tyler didn't know if the truth would make it worse or assure her that Brooke's safety was of the utmost importance to her. "There's one in every room." Tyler turned and looked at them.

"Isn't that a bit much?"

Tyler wasn't going to win with Janice. Luckily, Calvin interrupted. "Janice. Stop. We have guns locked up in our house, too. It's just a safety precaution."

Tyler needed to get out of this room. The walls were closing in on her. "I'm going to go take a shower. Please, help yourself to whatever you like. Make yourselves comfortable and all that."

She was in her bedroom before either had a chance to say a word to her. Tyler could feel her pulse pounding in the back of her head. She had taken on terrorists with rocket launchers at the ready, rappelled into buildings on rescue missions, she had been shot, even stabbed, but none of those experiences had anything on Janice Hart. *Al-Qaida should really recruit her.*

As soon as she closed the door, she pulled out her phone and saw Brooke's text.

My parents will be there when you get home. Please don't let my mom get under your skin. I'll be there ASAP. I love you.

Tyler tossed the phone on the bed. Now she was irritated with Brooke because she couldn't be irritated with Brooke. Her first thought was to hunker down in her bedroom until Brooke got home. She looked around at her furniture, thinking she could make a substantial barricade in front of her door. *What's wrong with you? This could be your future mother-in-law. Suck it up, Marine.* That's when she heard her voice from the other room, speaking at a volume sure to reach Tyler through the walls.

"I don't know how these two survive. There is nothing of sustenance here."

Tyler clenched her jaw and thought again about the barricade. Instead, she steeled her will and started pulling off her clothes, heading for the longest shower she could possibly take.

CHAPTER SIX

Caden made her fourth pass by the room where Rowen was being held. She paced the hallway, not completely sure what her next move should be. She knew something was off with Rowen, and the fact that she couldn't figure it out was driving her crazy. She had a suspicion that if she could get in the room alone with her, she could get her to talk. Rowen had been ogling her before, and maybe she could use that to get to the truth. She would normally have run the idea past Tyler, and they would have worked out a plan together. Caden didn't feel like she could take that approach this time, though. Tyler would have been adamantly against it. She would have said it was crossing a line. *And she would have been right. What is wrong with you? Are you trying to get fired? Or worse, obtain information illegally?* Caden turned down the hall to exit the building when she came face-to-face with Jennifer.

"What are you doing here?" Caden knew she'd come off more brash than she had intended, but she was caught off guard. And if she was honest with herself, she was a little embarrassed by what she had been considering. Seeing Jennifer was a reminder that she was the type of person who would consider using sexual prowess to get information.

Jennifer assumed her defensive position, crossing her arms and tilting her head a bit. Caden knew the look all too well.

"I'm coming to get you out of here before you get yourself into trouble. What the hell are you doing down here?" Jennifer's blue eyes were shimmering with anger and irritation.

Caden imitated her stance, crossing her arms. "I'm checking on Rowen…or I mean, the prisoner."

Jennifer grabbed her upper arm and pulled her down the hallway. She pushed her out of the door and into another seemingly identical hallway. "What is your problem?"

Caden didn't like the feeling of being reprimanded and pulled her arm loose. "You're my only problem right now. We captured her, and I was coming to check on her. Why are you acting like a jealous girlfriend?"

Jennifer leaned close to whisper in her ear. Caden wasn't sure if she was doing it not to be heard by anyone who could be nearby, or to articulate her annoyance. You never knew with her.

"Rowen Knight is not who you think she is, and you need to stay away from her until the briefing you will be receiving later today." She pulled away and stared at Caden with the hostility that only a scorned woman could muster. "And don't flatter yourself." She brushed her dark bangs out of her eyes.

Part of Caden was grateful that Jennifer was trying to look out for her; the other part was a bit hurt that she still brushed off their night together with such ease. Caden pushed past her, though she wasn't sure where she was headed. But she always liked getting the last word in, especially with Jennifer. "Your adoration is noted."

Caden made it to the locker room where a few cots were set up haphazardly. She walked over to one, pulled her shoes off, and fell backward onto the lumpy, makeshift bed. She stared at the ceiling and allowed her mind to wander. *Jennifer. Hmpft.* She rolled onto her side and closed her eyes, letting her mind travel back to a night, just a few months ago. It was still so vivid…

The sky had been dark, and the air had been bitterly cold. The kind of cold that bit at your bones and prickled your skin.

Caden was in the process of cursing the East Coast winter that was keeping her from running outside. It had chained her to a treadmill, which she loathed, and even more so, it had kept her inside in general. The walls were closing in. She had been staring out the window of her one-bedroom apartment when she'd seen a familiar person pass below. There wasn't much on this block, and there could only be one place she was heading, the bar that was nicely placed about two hundred feet from her door. Caden had grabbed her coat and headed out the door, willing to brave the harsh, frigid air, if only for a bit of company and banter.

Once inside the bar, she'd been able to locate her immediately. Jennifer sat at a table by herself, sipping a glass of wine. Caden noticed her posture and thought that most people wouldn't have been that comfortable sitting alone, but Jennifer was. She was confident and independent. She didn't attempt to look preoccupied with staring at her phone. She just sat there with her thoughts. Thoughts that had seemed a bit heavy, given the expression on her face.

Caden was normally confident in her interactions with women. She had no issue reading them, anticipating their needs, wants, and desires, even if she was only doing it for a night. The issue with Jennifer was that her normal approach was consistently blown off. At first, Caden had assumed it was because Jennifer was straight. But then there were moments, just passing seconds, where she could sense the attraction between them. She knew Jennifer had a thing for her, even if she wasn't acknowledging it, and it intrigued Caden to the point she needed to know what it was all about.

Caden had bought herself a drink and a glass of wine for Jennifer. She made it to the table and sat down. She'd slid the glass of red wine across and given Jennifer her most charming smile. "Mind if I join you?"

Jennifer had seemed to fight back a smile. "As if I have a choice."

"There is always a choice. I think you're smart enough to make the right one."

"Does that always work?"

"What?"

"The cool, elusive, angle?"

Caden had held in her laugh. She'd sipped out of the bottle of beer that she held in her hand and then set it back on the table. "Yes."

Jennifer sipped her wine. "It won't on me."

Caden had tipped her beer in Jennifer's direction, intrigued as ever but not willing to show it. "Noted."

They talked, laughed, and teased for well over an hour. Caden had enjoyed seeing that side of her. Jennifer had started to let her guard down a bit and was letting Caden see a side of her that wasn't tied to work. She'd caught herself staring on more than one occasion at the way Jennifer's hair fell across her face when she was in the middle of describing a story that took all of her attention. She'd enjoyed the way she accentuated her humor with her blue eyes, allowing them to light up with excitement. She'd enjoyed everything about her.

It didn't take all that long before they had both had far too much to drink, and the room became a backdrop for just the two of them. The voices and noises became muted, and Caden had felt as if there were no one else in the world.

"I want to go home with you." Jennifer had made the statement with such confidence and assurance; she didn't leave any room for argument. Or at least that's what Caden had told herself. She hadn't wanted to talk herself out of it because at that moment, there wasn't anything she had wanted more.

Several sex laden, orgasm filled hours later, Caden lay staring at Jennifer, who was sleeping deeply. The sky was just starting its daily transformation from night to day. A sliver of light provided just enough illumination to make out the features on Jennifer's sleeping face. Caden had always found Jennifer attractive, but not necessarily beautiful. Not until this moment, on this morning. Caden moved her hand slowly up to Jennifer's face. She touched the wisp of hair that had fallen across her eyes, and she pushed it back.

Her touch had woken Jennifer. Her eyes had opened and she'd focused on Caden. Her reaction to Caden, however, wasn't what Caden had expected. She'd jumped out of bed and started making excuses for having spent the night in her arms. She'd dressed with even more fervor than she had undressed. She'd apologized, reiterated a hundred more times that it was a mistake, and was gone.

Caden had called several times, but Jennifer avoided her at all costs. In fact, she purposely went out of her way to not run into Caden at all. Caden had played this very game several times. It was just that, a game, but one that didn't have a clear winner. Usually, she was the one not to return calls and to avoid people in the hallway. It hurt her more than she liked to admit, though she'd never say it out loud. Especially to Jennifer. When they finally did have to have a conversation, Caden kept it light and acted like nothing had ever happened. That was clearly what Jennifer wanted, and she was happy to oblige. She didn't need that kind of drama, and she sure as hell didn't want to be some straight girl's experiment. It didn't matter that it had been the best sex of her life, and that a bit of emotion had seeped in as well. Nope. That didn't matter one bit.

Caden flopped over on her other side, resigned to not letting Jennifer back into her head, if even for a moment. She felt the heat rise from her neck and up to her ears. No one quite got under her skin the way that cocky little computer jockey did. Caden shook her head; she needed to focus on something else. Luckily for her, there was plenty going on at work to help divert her attention. She finally started to drift off to sleep with images of aerial maps and sniper positions flashing through her mind.

CHAPTER SEVEN

I understand that you're only here for a few days, but I'm completely exhausted. I worked all night long. Can I just get a few hours of sleep and we'll come meet you for lunch?" Brooke had been arguing for the last twenty-five minutes with her mother, and she was starting to hit her breaking point. She was tired, frustrated, and worried about how all of this was affecting Tyler. She hadn't had the opportunity to discuss the matter privately with Tyler yet, but she could see the tension in the way she sat, in her movements, in her eyes.

"Who is we?"

Brooke's mother was usually the most politically correct and tactful person Brooke had ever met. The fact that she was referencing Tyler with such disdain was not only infuriating, it was also very out of character. "*We* is Tyler and me. You know, the blonde who has been so patiently and quietly sitting on the couch listening to you berate me for the last half hour. Tyler, my girlfriend. Who lives with me. The woman I love, who I've told you about a hundred times."

"Brooke Lynn Hart. I will not have you speak to me that way, nor will I have you disrespect your father or me." Janice brushed little particles off her wool sleeves that weren't there. She had performed this very motion for as long as Brooke could remember. It was her mother's way of saying *I'm done talking about this.*

Brooke rolled her eyes and decided her last-ditch effort would be to plead with her father. He never said much, but what he said was always final. "Dad, please. I'll meet you at one o'clock. We can go to that Italian place you like down on F Street."

Her father seemed to think about it for a moment and then pushed himself off the couch. He went over to Brooke and kissed her forehead. "Sure thing, sweetheart. See you then." He looked over at Tyler for a moment, seemingly to size her up. His facial expressions had never been very easy to read. His eyes, on the other hand, never lied. Brooke knew his eyes were her own. But right now, she couldn't decipher what was in them. It could have been disappointment, but she could also just be projecting her mother onto him.

"Gunnery Sergeant." He nodded at her.

Tyler stood and mirrored his motion. "Sir."

Her dad took her mom's hand and pulled her toward the door. "Let's go, Janice. We can see Brooke in a bit."

Her mom had never made a habit of arguing with her dad, and apparently, today she wasn't going to deviate from her norm. Brooke was thankful. As the door shut behind them, she let out a sigh of relief. Tyler was next to her immediately, wrapping her in a reassuring hug.

"I'm so sorry about that." She talked into Tyler's neck as she fought back the tears. "I know it's been a long night. That's the last thing you needed to deal with."

Tyler rubbed her back. It felt good, calming, and it was needed. "If the whole 'heading up charities' thing doesn't work out, your mom could go to work for us as an interrogation specialist." She laughed, then her tone became more serious. "You should meet them for lunch. I just came back to sleep for a bit and then I need to head back."

Brooke didn't move from her position. Being nestled against Tyler was the most secure place she had ever known. "I need to go back too, and I want to find out everything I can about this—"

Tyler cut her off. "There will still be plenty for you to do after lunch. You should meet your parents. If for no other reason than to keep them from showing back up here, unannounced."

Brooke squeezed a little tighter. "I'm sorry about my mom."

Tyler kissed the top of her head. "Don't be. She'll adjust." But Tyler's voice didn't reflect her words. Brooke knew she didn't fully believe the statement either.

Brooke didn't respond. What she didn't want to tell Tyler was that Janice Hart never *adjusted* to anything without a fight. She was a career military wife who has the perseverance of a Greek warrior and the stubbornness of a mule. In her mom's world, everything needed to be perfect, or at the very least appear perfect. She had never fully accepted Brooke's sexuality, and Brooke didn't believe that stance would change anytime soon.

"Your dad seemed nice."

Brooke chuckled. "I have heard my father described in many different ways. I'm not sure that *nice* has ever been one of them."

Tyler gave Brooke a tight squeeze before she broke their embrace and started toward the bedroom. "He's your dad, Brooke. I'm going to give him the benefit of the doubt."

Brooke followed closely behind. "Always the optimist."

Tyler sat on the bed. "It's not about being optimistic, it's about being realistic. You told me yourself that you came out to your parents in high school."

Brooke sat next to her, putting her head on her shoulder. "I also told you that they refused to accept it then, and clearly, not much has changed."

"Except that now you're an adult." Tyler took her hand, intertwining their fingers. "They see us together, here in our home, happy."

Tyler's ability to compartmentalize issues typically helped give Brooke clarity when she was lacking the capacity to do so for herself. However, in this instance, it was blinding her. "It's not that simple. They don't see what you and I see, what we feel. They see what they want to see."

"And what is that?"

"That their only daughter is shacked up with a woman. A woman that will never be good enough because she's...well, a woman."

Tyler's body stiffened, and Brooke shifted so she could look at her. Tyler stared at the ground, looking defeated and hurt. "I'm not always going to be a special agent. I hope to be a director, eventually."

The words hurt Brooke's heart, not because they weren't true, but because Tyler felt like she needed to say them aloud. "Oh, honey." She kissed her cheek. "I didn't mean to imply that you're not good enough. You're more than enough. You're so much more than I ever hoped for, more than I deserve."

"Not to them."

"Good thing I don't care what they think."

Tyler stood, breaking their contact. "Are you sure about that? I don't come from your world, Brooke. I didn't go to fancy schools. I don't have a trust fund. I don't have vacation homes in different parts of the world."

Brooke wasn't sure how to react. Tyler rarely responded emotionally. She was always the picture of composure. She was the rational one, the part of their pair that kept them balanced, centered. "Is that really what you think I care about?"

Tyler put her hands on her hips, a pose of defiance and defensiveness. "We've never talked about what that means for our future. When the dust settles and the novelty of me wears off, when you realize that I don't fit into the world you were raised in, the one you're comfortable in, where will I fit in then?"

Brooke put her hand on her arm. She wanted her full attention, and she knew touch was the best way to get that with Tyler. "Tyler, I'm not part of that world. Yes, I was raised in it, but it's not what I chose. I chose to go work for the CIA. I chose not to participate in the rhetoric. I chose to be with you, and I choose that every day."

Tears formed in Tyler's eyes. "What if one day you change your mind?"

Brooke was shocked into silence. Picturing her world without Tyler in it wasn't conceivable. There wasn't a version of her future where that possibility ever came to fruition. She'd pictured Tyler there with her every step of the way. The gravity of that realization sat on Brooke's chest, pushing down, squeezing her tightly. Did Tyler not know what she meant to her? Had she not made herself perfectly clear? She could hear her voice cracking as she spoke. "Tyler, I love you. I don't ever want to be without you. If I haven't made that perfectly clear by now, I'm sorry. I don't just want you in my life, I need you in it."

Thankfully, the words seemed to reach Tyler. She pulled Brooke against her, melding their bodies together. She kissed the side of Brooke's head. "I love you. I'm sorry. I don't mean to doubt you. I don't know what your mother does to me."

Brooke was used to her mother's effortless malice. "She has that effect on everyone." She squeezed Tyler harder, attempting to wring out any doubt that remained. Brooke had grown accustomed to the belittling and coldness that her mother exuded whenever she felt the need, but Tyler didn't deserve this. Tyler, who had come to mean everything to Brooke, who had become the central piece to everything that was good in her life, was being treated like a disease that needed curing. It hurt Brooke to know she had any part in Tyler's pain, even if it was only through a shared bloodline.

CHAPTER EIGHT

Jennifer placed the empty cup next to her mouse. It was her fifth, no, sixth cup at this point. Most people's hands would be shaking from the surge of caffeine, but hers were still steady as her fingertips flew over the keyboard. The constant tapping was a comforting and familiar sound. She should have gone to bed hours ago, but she'd never be able to sleep with so much going on in her head.

She glanced at the eighty-inch monitor to her left. Rowen Knight was still moving around inside her room, pacing from wall to wall, and it looked like she was counting her steps. Jennifer mentally compared her to a caged animal, stalking across its cage. She moved the joystick, and the camera zoomed in on the animal's face.

Rowen had haphazardly pulled up her vibrant red hair, and loose strands still covered parts of her face. But even the slightly disheveled look didn't take away from her striking features. *Rowen. What kind of name is Rowen anyway? I bet she even has perfect teeth.* Jennifer zoomed the camera in a little farther. Rowen did a series of stretches and then dropped to the ground, taking a perfect push-up position. As if on cue, she looked up and smiled at the camera. Jennifer leaned back feeling as if she had just been caught spying. *Yup, perfect teeth. Well, that's annoying.*

This whole situation had her on high alert. It wasn't just that their pursuit of Lark had finally taken a turn, one that should help them immensely. And it wasn't just that Caden and Tyler had been in the line of fire again. Hell, she was used to that. Those two seemed to be on an endless quest for an adrenaline surge. They had been on at least four different missions in just the last few months. Jennifer had sat next to Brooke for each one, being the picture of support. She never wanted to admit to needing to be there as well, trying to squelch her own nerves about their fate. Of course she was concerned for Tyler's safety, but what she never wanted to admit was the way her heart lurched watching Caden walk out the door as well.

No, it was the way Caden had looked at Rowen. Caden was a bit reckless, and Rowen had knowledge of what was going on inside Lark's camp. Rowen could be the key to finally catching that bastard, but Caden could barely keep her tongue in her mouth when looking at her. Jennifer let out a hiss. *It's not jealousy. I'm just looking out for my friend, that's all.* Her egotistical, mouthy, reckless, painfully attractive friend.

She leaned back in her chair and stared at the ceiling. The same ceiling she had stared at the morning after she had awoken in Caden's bed and made a mad dash for the office, her safe zone. It was still the same. Stark white ceiling tiles with tiny dots, harsh fluorescent lights in perfectly equal distances. There hadn't been answers in the dots that morning, just as there were no answers in them today. She chewed on her bottom lip and remembered.

She'd known exactly what she had been doing that night. She had her wits about her when she asked Caden to take her home, and she knew exactly what she was doing when she had fallen into bed with her. Sure, maybe the alcohol had made it a little easier to voice what she wanted, but it hadn't been the catalyst for what had happened later. That night with Caden had been intimate, passionate, and eye-opening. She had always appraised women from afar but had never touched one the way she'd touched Caden that night. Hell, she'd never been touched by *anyone* the way Caden had touched her. Caden was strong and soft all at the same time. She was powerful and gentle. Intense, yet comforting. It had all been so overwhelming, and in the light of day it had been too much to process. Jennifer knew when she had woken up to those dark, dreamy eyes that she wasn't going to process anything, not correctly anyway. So she ran. She said it had been a mistake, a drunken misstep. She knew that wasn't true. It was a lie that she told herself to shield her heart from the inevitable pain that would come with falling for Caden Styles. It was a lie she continued to tell herself every time she looked at her. A lie that she had told so often, she should believe it by now. But she didn't. Not for a single second. There wasn't a single instance where she came into contact with Caden that she didn't want to touch her, feel her, or be near her. Of course, this usually came out in an aggressive manner, expressed through sarcastic comments and eye rolls. She groaned, disappointed with herself. *I'm pretty much a teenage boy. Nice.*

Jennifer was dragged away from her self-loathing by a change in the exercise routine on the screen. Rowen had flipped over the chair and was now doing dips on it. *You've got to be kidding me.* She pushed herself up and down with the amount of effort Jennifer used to brush her hair. *Is this woman for real?* Oh, she was real. Very real, very beautiful, and very much on Caden's radar. *Perfect.* She looked down at her body, slouched over in her chair. She poked at her breasts and then looked at the taut, muscular chest on the screen. She grabbed her small belly roll through her shirt and compared it to the tight, flat stomach of the woman who had apparently decided she needed only to be in a sports bra now. She touched her plain brown hair and wondered if Rowen's vibrant red was her natural color. She let out an aggravated grunt and decided that there was only one thing for her to do. She got out of her chair and headed down to the cafeteria for breakfast.

❖

A few hours had passed too quickly. Brooke's sleep had been broken and sporadic. The only reason she hadn't gotten out of bed was the possessive and comforting hold that Tyler had on her. Brooke aimlessly dragged her fingers up and down Tyler's arm. It was bad enough her parents had dropped in suddenly for a visit, but her mother's clear and offensive dismissal of Tyler wasn't something she would soon forgive. Brooke's anger continued to rise. It began as a burning sensation that started in her chest and crept its way up through her chest and then her face. She could feel the burning sensation through her neck and ears. She tried to think of a time where she had been this upset…no, this disappointed with her mother. There was no anecdote for comparison, which made her more upset. Her phone vibrated, distracting her from her growing agitation. She grabbed at it and opened the message. *Briefing at fifteen hundred hours.* Good. At least that was an excuse to leave after lunch. Her parents, well, at least her father, wouldn't protest.

She rolled over and stared at Tyler. Her slow, rhythmic breathing indicated that she was deeply asleep, something that she desperately needed. Brooke fought back the urge to touch her face. As sound asleep as Tyler appeared, she was always just one slight movement away from being completely awake. She wasn't going to take this sleep away from her. Tyler's sleep patterns had improved, but they were far from where Brooke would like to see them. The nightmares were still there, the psychological scars most apparent when Tyler drifted into dreamland. She took in Tyler's body. The memories of war and battles fought left their marks in the form of roughly healed skin, proving the past would always leave its mark.

"I can hear you staring at me."

Brooke smiled. "That doesn't even make sense."

Tyler opened her eyes, looking fully awake. "What's wrong?"

Brooke didn't want to bring up the subject of her parents again, knowing the pain it would bring Tyler. "I'm wondering why you still insist on sleeping in these ugly green tank tops."

Tyler looked down her chest. "I thought you liked these. You said they show off my muscles."

"No. I told you that I like taking them off you."

"You like taking everything off me." She grinned.

Brooke smiled and put her hand on the side of Tyler's face as she tried to swallow past overwhelming emotions. "You know that I love you. It doesn't matter what my parents say. You're it."

Tyler's eyes were so kind. She was able to say so much with them, without ever having to say a word. Right now, they were saying that she believed her and loved her. "It will be okay."

"Easy for you to say. I have to sit with them for an hour. You get to go to work."

Tyler leaned over and kissed her forehead. She left her mouth there for a long moment, reiterating what her eyes had already told her. "I'm only a phone call away."

"I know."

"Always," Tyler murmured as she pulled Brooke to her.

"Always."

Brooke knew Tyler meant what she said; she always did. What she didn't want to tell her was that her mother was a force to be reckoned with when she didn't get her way. Brooke hoped that always would *always* be enough.

CHAPTER NINE

B rooke was ten minutes early to her lunch date with her parents, but she knew they would already be there. Her father was fifteen minutes early to everything. Fifteen minutes early was on time and actually on time was late. She wasn't sure what waited for her behind those glass doors, and she wasn't sure she was mentally prepared to deal with her mother's badgering, but here she was.

The white tablecloths that lined every table, paired with the basic brown chairs, were nothing to write home about. People didn't flock to this place for its décor. They came because the food was incredible. Her father made it a point to eat at this restaurant, at the same table, every single time he was in town. At least the scenery would be familiar, which was slightly comforting.

As she approached the table, her father stood. His career military bearing shone through his posture and perfect stance. He kissed her cheek and pulled out her chair. Her mother gave her a brief and forced smile. Brooke had seen it before. It was the same smile she reserved for the certain woman that ran in her social circle, someone her mom didn't like or respect. The realization was painful, far more so than Brooke would have thought.

"Hi, Mom."

"Brooke." Her mother was straining to sound polite.

Brooke took her seat at the table, feeling like a seven-year-old girl all over again. She tried to push the feeling away, reminding herself that she was an adult.

"How's work?" her father asked, seeming genuinely interested. Unlike her mom, her dad seemed to take a real interest in Brooke's chosen career. She had enjoyed their conversations since she'd taken her spot at the CIA. It wasn't until then that her father had gone out of his way to call her.

"It's good." She tried to sound upbeat and positive, not wanting to give her mother an opening to attack her career choice as well. "We're working on something really important right now. I'll need to go to work right after lunch."

Her mom let out a long, annoyed sigh. "I still don't understand why you decided to work there. You could've done anything. You could've been anyone."

So much for not giving her an opening. Brooke wanted to stay quiet. She specifically told herself not to respond. Her natural defenses, though, wouldn't allow it. "What you mean is, I could have chosen to be with a man and stayed home like a good wife."

Her mom shifted in her seat. She grabbed the glass of red wine perched at the end of the table. "I had no desire to discuss such things this afternoon, Brooke. But since you brought it up." Her passive-aggressive tone, annunciating each word, was something her mother had perfected in her fifty-six years. "You don't honestly believe that Taylor...or whatever her name is, is a suitable partner."

Brooke willed her hands not to ball up in frustration. She had been practicing this technique with her mother for years and had become something of an expert. "Her name is *Tyler,* Mom. But you knew that since I've talked to you about her on several occasions." Her voice was calm, steady. She was impressed with herself.

The server brought over a glass of water for Brooke and asked if they were ready to order. Her mom ordered a salad, as she always did. Her father ordered the lasagna, just as he always did. Brooke stared blankly at the server. She couldn't believe they were so predictable and so callous all at the same time. In one breath, they were berating her life choices and ordering food in the next, as if it were the most natural thing in the world.

"I'm not hungry," Brooke told the server, who looked distinctly uncomfortable.

"Oh, Brooke, don't be dramatic." Her mom used a condescending tone Brooke knew all too well.

Brooke stared at her. "What would please you then, Mom? Do you want me to tell you that Tyler is a phase? Do you want to hear that I'm just biding my time, waiting for a knight in shining armor to come along?"

"I believe that Tyler *is* a phase."

Brooke laughed. It was an inappropriate and rather loud laugh, but that was the point. Her mother hated public shows of emotion, and Brooke really wanted to make her uncomfortable right now. "I came out to you in high school and yet you still act like this is breaking news."

Her dad cleared his throat. "Watch your tone, young lady."

Brooke switched her gaze over to her father. "Dad. You always told me that you wanted me to be happy. You wanted me to find someone that was kind, strong, smart, and did the right thing. Well, I did find that person, and it's Tyler."

Her dad stared at her contemplatively. Brooke imagined that it was partially because he was caught off guard by her reaction. Brooke typically fell in line, doing what was asked of her without question. She wasn't going to do that this time, not when it came to Tyler.

"Yes, Brooke, that is what I've always told you. That's still no reason to speak to your mother that way."

"I wouldn't need to speak this way if you two listened to me. I'm happy, and I'm in love. With Tyler."

"Stop saying that, Brooke." Her mother was starting to get angry.

"No, Mom, I won't. I'm not a child anymore, and in case you haven't realized it, your approval isn't necessary. I'm perfectly capable of being happy without it." Brooke wasn't sure, but she thought she saw tears starting to form in her mom's eyes. It could have been from anger. Brooke had never seen her mom cry.

"I don't want this life for you, Brooke. We didn't send you to the best schools we could find, spending thousands of dollars on your education, for you to end up here."

"End up where, Mom? In a job that I enjoy and with a person that I love? That's not where you wanted me to end up?"

"You know what I mean, Brooke. Don't try to change my words around."

Brooke was angry and hurt. She couldn't hide it anymore, nor did she want to, and she hadn't been doing a very good job anyway. "No. I don't think I do understand. Please explain it to me. Where, exactly, did you not want me to end up?"

Her mom sipped her wine and set it back on the table. After a moment of uncomfortable silence, she said softly, "We won't have a lesbian for a daughter."

Brooke couldn't do anything but stare. Her heart hurt. More than that, something inside her broke. She took a sip of her water and shifted the napkin on the table before getting up. "I've been out to you for years. I don't know why you're suddenly deciding this now. But I guess I'm no longer your daughter." She got up to leave. She expected her legs to be shaky, but they were strong and steadfast beneath her. Her family unit, as dysfunctional as it might be, was crashing around her, but at least her body wasn't betraying her.

Her father stood as well. "Brooke, please. Let's all sit down and talk about this."

She stared at him. She wanted him to say that her mom didn't speak for both of them, that he felt differently. But he didn't. She looked into the eyes that matched her own. She saw a twinge of something, but she didn't know what it was. She couldn't be here any longer. She turned and went toward the door. Each step burned with rejection, with the knowledge that she was a disappointment for being who she was, and worse, that her happiness meant she'd lose the people who were supposed to love her unconditionally. She got in her car and let the tears stream down her face as she headed to work, where people valued who she was and what she did.

❖

Tyler was trying to figure out why these two men were sitting at their meeting table. It wasn't a typical occurrence for the director of Homeland Security to sit in on one of these meetings. Nor was it a normal occurrence for the director of the CIA, but here they both were. They had entered the room just moments before the meeting was set to begin. They had taken their seats at the end of the table, nodding recognition to their staff as they passed by. Their black suits were impeccable. They had a shiny quality about them, identifying the expensive quality.

Caden sat next to Tyler, just as she usually did. Caden seemed uneasy. She was fidgeting with her hands and constantly shifting in her seat. It was totally unlike her, and Tyler doubted very much that it was due to the presence of their bosses, since that type of thing didn't normally put Caden on edge.

Tyler looked across the table at Brooke and Jennifer. Jennifer looked tired, worn out. She clearly needed rest. Brooke's eyes were dark, almost haunted, and it looked like she'd been crying. Tyler tried to remember a time that she had seen them like that before, and nothing came to mind. Something was wrong. She wanted to pull her out of the room and talk to her. She wanted to know what was going on. *It must be her damn parents.* Tyler's chest burned with pain for Brooke, and she hated not being able to do anything about it.

Rezentes, who was already standing at the front of the room, adjusted his suit. He was one of the biggest kiss-asses that she had ever known. His priorities lay with impressing the men that sat at the other end of the table. It was never with the mission or with national security; it was for his glorification and advancement. He was disgusting.

"Rowen Knight's files have been released to us. She is exactly who I presumed she would be."

Tyler fought the urge to roll her eyes. Rezentes didn't know shit. He was a poor excuse for a leader and an even poorer excuse for a CIA employee. He had no natural instincts and portrayed information that his team was able to gather for him as his own. She kept her calm, knowing that making an enemy of him would just make her job harder.

"She's French Intelligence. She'd been working undercover, gathering information for her government. Her assignment was to gain access to Lark and his organization."

The CIA director, who had a monotone, deep voice said, "All of this is in the briefing paperwork, which I assume everyone here has read. Please get to mission objectives. We don't have all day."

Tyler liked him.

Rezentes looked flustered. His face flushed red, and he cleared his throat. "Yes, well…we've been given permission to use her in a joint task force. The objective will be to continue to gain access to Lark's operation. All information will be shared between the United States and French governments, as both have vested interests. She's been playing Lark's side for a while, attempting to gain the organization's trust. That type of time isn't something we can replicate. We're to work together on this. Knight has been out of contact for quite some time with her government, which happens once a spy goes deep undercover. What that means is that we aren't sure exactly where she stands and we have to take her word at face value. Her reputation with the

French government is solid, but we aren't even sure at this point why they're involved with Lark at all."

The director of Homeland Security cut him off. "Styles and Monroe, you're to work with Knight. Help her and keep an eye on her. I'll leave the details to you, but I want regular briefings. We need to get this situation resolved as quickly as possible. Find out what she knows, and do it fast."

Tyler paid attention to the way he chose to phrase the word situation. *Such a politician.* She was continuously amazed by the way he was able to refer to Lark and the homegrown terrorist organization as a "situation." Everyone knew this had the potential to become one of the biggest catastrophes on American soil, achieved by American people. The thought sent chills through her body, and she couldn't help but look at Brooke. Her safe place, her home.

Brooke looked like she was listening. To anyone else sitting in the room, she was the picture of perfect attention, but Tyler knew better. Something was wrong. Brooke made eye contact briefly, and then her focus shifted back to the front of the room.

Rezentes, never wanting to be one-upped, added his input. "Analysts Hart and Glass will be at your disposal."

Tyler knew it pained him to say it. Rezentes believed the CIA was superior to Homeland, and the fact that they wouldn't be running lead on this must have burned his ass.

Both the directors seemed pleased with the resolution, and they got up and left the room. They nodded to Rezentes as they walked past, which obviously played to his ego. He was acting like a dog who had just been rewarded for not taking a crap on the carpet. His eyes filled with macho ego.

Caden stood, and Rezentes took it as an affront. "You weren't dismissed, Special Agent."

Caden barely looked at him. "We don't answer to you, Rezentes, and we have to get to work."

"I want a briefing as well." He had to get the last word.

Caden continued toward the door. "You can get that from your analysts."

Tyler was right behind her. She didn't need to participate in this verbal battle. Caden was speaking for both of them, and that was fine with her. Passing Brooke without being able to talk to her was painful, though. She wanted to check on her, but now wasn't the time. And drawing any attention to their relationship in front of Rezentes was just asking for trouble neither of them needed. They headed toward the interrogation room, and though Tyler wondered what Caden was thinking, she didn't want to intrude on her thoughts. She'd share when she was ready.

Tyler peered through the small window of the room. Rowen was pacing, and Tyler knew the innate motion all too well. Rowen was French Intelligence, a spy, and the idle repetitiveness she had been placed in was probably grating on her nerves. *Good.* Tyler knew what the briefing reports said, but it didn't change the fact that she didn't trust her. There was still more to the story than any of them knew, and until Tyler felt as if she had the full story laid out in front of her, she wouldn't be cutting her any slack.

She pushed the door open, forcing Rowen to give her full attention to the only activity in the room.

"We know who you are," Tyler said.

"Then you know we're on the same side."

Tyler laughed. "I don't know that. All I know is we caught you when we were looking for our target, and when we got you, you failed to tell us who you really are."

Rowen shoved her hands in her pockets, neither her posture nor her stare giving anything away. "I wanted you to catch me."

"Yes. But why?" Tyler didn't want to play any more games; she wanted answers.

"So I could keep my cover intact. Isn't that more beneficial for us?" Her posture loosened slightly when Caden came up beside Tyler.

Tyler noticed the change but didn't have time to explore the reasoning. "What do you know?"

Rowen pulled the khaki colored shirt off the back of the chair and pulled it on over her white tank top. She moved to the door and waited expectantly.

"Where do you think you're going?" Caden snapped at her.

Most women would have flinched at the harsh tone Caden had tossed her way, but not Rowen. She gave them a cocky smile. "Take me to your information center and I'll brief you."

Tyler could sense Caden's impatience. She was going to need to reel this in, but not in front of Rowen. There couldn't be a crack in their united front. "Okay. Follow me."

Tyler pulled the door open, and Rowen stopped in the doorway, her eyes fixed on Caden. "I'm looking forward to working with you, Special Agent."

Caden didn't respond, but she didn't need to say anything. Tyler saw her jaw clench as Rowen walked past. *What the hell is her problem?*

❖

Caden followed Rowen, with Tyler leading. She wanted to get her senses about her, and to do that, she needed to make sure Rowen couldn't see her face. Rowen had her a bit unfocused, and that was dangerous. Distractions from the mission led to mistakes. Mistakes led to injury, or even worse, failure. None of those options were suitable outcomes. She had known Rowen wasn't exactly who she said she was, thanks to Jennifer's information, but she hadn't been anticipating French Intelligence. She couldn't shake the feeling that Rowen was being purposely obtuse. It didn't add up. She could have come clean once she was in custody, because she knew they would find out. Instead, she made them jump through hoops to find out what she could have told them anyway, even if they would have had to verify it. Caden wasn't entirely sure what she had expected, but it wasn't for Rowen to be a legitimate spy.

She took a silent, deep breath. They had to come up with a plan to catch Lark, once and for all. That was the bottom line, and that's where her focus needed to be. Whatever interest was bubbling between her and Rowen needed to be sidelined or forgotten. The latter was probably the better option.

Tyler placed her hand over the alarm sensor and the door beeped, indicating their entrance to the control room. Brooke and Jennifer were sitting in front of their computers. Dozens of documents, pictures, and maps were on the large screens at the front of the room. Jennifer and Brooke stood when the three of them entered the room. Rezentes was sitting in one of the corners. He had a scowl on his face, as usual. Caden fought back the urge to wink at him. Instead, she turned her attention to Jennifer, whose eyes were already on her. Caden usually enjoyed the feeling of Jennifer looking at her. A few times, she thought she could feel her skin burning where her eyes had traveled moments before. Right now, though, the intensity wasn't coming from a place of desire or longing. It was angry, accusatory.

Brooke wasted no time as the three of them took a seat, and everyone focused on the screens. "I'm Analyst Hart, and this is Analyst Glass. We're here to help in any way we can. Let me tell you what we know."

Rowen didn't seem to care about the disgruntled man sitting in the corner. She simply nodded at Brooke and Jennifer. "Can I ask why there's only three of you assigned to this?"

"The fewer people that are involved, the better." Rezentes ignored the fact that the question wasn't addressed to him and strode over to Rowen. His face had shifted slightly. His expression was softer, almost kind. His voiced warmed and seemed... flirtatious. "We don't know how far this reaches, and the people in this room have been extensively vetted. We're the only ones that we can trust." He sat on the corner of Rowen's table and put out his hand.

Caden didn't hide her eye roll. She watched as he attempted to flirt with Rowen, his stomach pushing out the buttons on his white shirt. His hair was slicked back, which only accentuated his receding hairline. Rowen took his hand but barely looked at him, her attention still on the screens.

"That's not right." She pointed to one of the maps. "That access road you have highlighted isn't the one they use." She moved to the screen, where she pointed at various sections. "They use an underground tunnel for almost all of their transportation and storage." She turned and faced them. "Much of what has been built was to intentionally confuse you. He's aware he's being watched."

Caden listened. Unfortunately, what she noticed was that this was the first inkling of an accent that she had heard Rowen use. She stared harder, forcing herself to pay attention.

"From the intel I gathered, there are several other small camps like this one." She pointed to Jennifer, who was sitting at one of the computer stations. "Zoom in."

Jennifer did as she was told. Rowen directed her for a few moments. "There." She pointed. "There's a small access point that leads to the underground camp they've created. Honestly, it's very impressive."

Tyler had been taking notes. "How many of these underground camps are there?"

Rowen shrugged. "It's hard to say for sure, but at least four. Not all of them are underground either. This main one is. That one they seem to use as their headquarters. It's the largest and most complex. From the intel I've been able to gather, the others are outposts of sorts. They pop up when needed as drop off and pickup locations for weapons or other equipment. They're typically located on private property. I haven't been able to get a name for any of the landowners, but I don't think any of them are involved. My best guess is that they pay in cash for temporary use of a small portion of the property for a limited amount of time, and once their business is complete, they move on."

Caden tried to picture the outposts, but it didn't make any sense to her. "How long do they stay on the property, and what are they telling these landowners?"

"No one knows the full story for sure, but the best I could put together is that they've created these outposts using small mobile homes. They approach landowners, offer them a sum of money to use a small corner of their property for a month. They move everything around in these homes, and to anyone paying attention, they're just nomads, moving from one location to the next. Once their business there is complete, they move on. Tracing them has been very difficult. They're able to go where they're needed and without much interference, if any, and they do it all completely off grid. Cash only, no cards."

Tyler stared, and Caden couldn't make out what she was thinking. "Which one of these outposts do we find Lark in?"

Rowen smiled. Much to Caden's irritation, she felt a spur of attraction jolt in her stomach. Irritated with herself, she tried to overcompensate by leaning forward, hoping to push the feeling aside.

"None of them. All of them. I don't know."

Tyler tapped her pen. "Okay." She had drawn out the vowels in her statement. "Where *can* we find him? We were able to pinpoint the location we found you at, an outpost as you call it, because of a tip we received from ATF. One of their informants gave them a lead on illegal gun sales, but the informant was sure it wasn't a typical sales ring. He thought it was much bigger, which is why they called us. Once we got there, as you know, all that was left was you. So, where exactly is Lark?"

"I've never been able to figure that out. The organization is set up ingeniously. Everyone knows just enough, but not so much that I could pinpoint who Lark was or where to find him. It's set up so that every four people report to two other people. They call that a pod. Half of the pod reports to one person while the other half reports to another. Those two people report to two different people. These people are not located in the same place. I believe they do this to compare information, to see which is more accurate. Those two people report via messages to a centralized location. That's where I lost track of how things work. There's a centralized location, from what I understand, where there's a computer mainframe. Where it goes from there is anyone's guess. But my assumption is that Lark downloads this information and then reverses the cycle when he wants something done. This eliminates the possibility of disseminating information that could lead to the location and identity of Lark. But the only thing that makes sense is that this centralized location is this underground camp." Rowen pointed to the largest outpost on the screen. "Lark is clearly paranoid, and he wants to be where he knows he's protected. The only place he can assure that protection is in a location where he controls every entrance and exit, with his security infrastructure and his people. The largest underground outpost has been set up like a rat's maze. It'll be practically impossible to penetrate without him knowing you're there. But the thing is, I'm pretty sure Lark isn't as high as it goes. The things these people are interested in, their mobility, their network…it seems to add up to much more than just one guy on some kind of mission. I'm just not sure what that *much more* is."

Rezentes was the only one that had an audible response. "Well, fuck."

Caden hated to admit it, but she agreed with Rezentes. Fuck was right.

Jennifer was staring at Caden. Caden was staring at Rowen. Well, to be fair, everyone was staring at Rowen. She was the one talking. It wasn't the fact that Caden was looking at her, it was the *way* she looked at her. Jennifer had seen that fire in Caden's eyes, when it had been directed at her. Her stomach turned.

Caden had the ability to make you feel as if you were the only person in the room. Her focus was intense, complete, and unwavering. Jennifer had never known she wanted to be the center of anyone's attention that way. She didn't even know that it was possible. Sure, she had heard about it, read about it, even seen it occur between Brooke and Tyler. She knew it existed. She just never thought it was a possibility for her. Now, it was all she could think about, especially as she watched the one person whose attention she wanted more than anything, giving it to someone else. *Her new target.* Jennifer hated herself for even thinking it. She never really believed she was a "target" for Caden. She knew what they had shared was genuine. She also knew that Caden's laser focus could change quickly and without warning. Jennifer felt chills roll through her body. Caden was done with her and was moving on. She needed to accept it.

Jennifer looked back at Rowen, who was explaining the way Lark's organization was designed. It was good information. It would be helpful. It would change the way they would pursue him, but all she wanted was for Rowen to stop speaking. Her subtle accent and hardened body were painfully alluring.

She hadn't noticed that Rowen had, in fact, stopped speaking until she finally pulled herself away from her internal thoughts and looked at the four faces staring at her, clearly waiting for an answer of some kind. An answer that she couldn't give because she had no idea what was asked.

"I'm sorry. What was that?"

Brooke's expression was one of concern. "Do you think we can get into the system?"

Jennifer took a moment to put the information she'd paid attention to into place. "Into Lark's system?"

Caden, with her always present smartass inclination, mocked her lapse of attention. "No. We were talking about hacking the cable company. Maybe we can all finally get HBO for free."

Normally, Jennifer would have a retort of equal measure for her, but she couldn't seem to clump her thoughts together. "I'll need some more specifics."

Rowen barely let her finish her sentence. "I'll help."

Jennifer felt her hand twitch. "Perfect." She would have rather stuck needles in her eyes than spend more time with Rowen, but there was no way around it now. Rowen knew more than anyone else they had ever encountered about Lark's organization. The only upside was that if Rowen was with her, she wasn't with Caden.

Caden pointed to the computer. "Pull up what we have."

Jennifer glanced over at Tyler, who looked like she was going to object. When Tyler said nothing, Jennifer did as she was asked.

Caden grabbed the remote off the table and pointed it toward the large screen. She pushed the button, and dozens of documents appeared on the screen, information they had been able to obtain on Lark over the last several months. "Nathanial Lark, currently the most wanted terrorist in America. He's forty-one years old, an only child, both parents are dead. We know he was born in Seattle, Washington, and graduated high school third in his class. He went to the University of Washington where he earned his bachelor's degree in engineering. While he was in college, he wrote a few papers regarding the decline of the white race in America. One of the papers was so disturbing it earned him a written letter of reprimand from the dean."

Although Jennifer knew all of this already, since she had put the information together, it still made her skin crawl hearing it out loud. She squeezed her hands together and continued to listen to Caden, who had flipped to a different set of pictures and more bullet points.

"After graduation, he moved around a bit, until he settled in Alabama and joined the National Socialist Movement. Currently, there are about four hundred members located in thirty-two states."

Brooke interjected. "Basically, he's a white supremacist."

Caden pulled up another image. "Yes, but an extremely intelligent one. In case you aren't familiar with the National Socialist Movement here in the United States, Rowen, they're neo-Nazis."

Jennifer watched Rowen, who momentarily changed her facial expression. She seemed confused for a second, and then hid whatever else she was thinking. Caden hadn't seemed to notice, and she continued her rundown.

"He moved up the ranks rather quickly, gaining power and influence. We can trace his rise to power through the editorials he has written in the National Socialist Movement periodicals and even in some mainstream newspapers. He never married, but his onetime girlfriend did give birth to a son. Chris Carlson Lark dropped the Lark once he entered school, and trained his whole life to help advance his father's thinking. He even managed to enter the CIA and make it through the majority of training until we figured it out and were able to stop him." She changed the picture of Carlson and continued. "These aren't your run-of-the-mill skinheads. They're smart, well funded, and have the ability to hide in plain sight. In fact, we don't have a single picture of Lark since college. What's even more troubling is the potential connections he has all over the world. At last count, the British National Party, although declining, still has representation. The Party claims they have upward of three thousand members, although official counts say about five hundred. We operate under the assumption that it's somewhere in the middle. The active party in France, the National Front, is even more troublesome. They're actually taking up six out of thirteen seats in the government and have gained support in their presidential elections. If there was ever an effort to join all these extremists, who knows what they could accomplish."

She put the clicker down and took a seat. "We just can't seem to put together what he's after. Trying to gain access to CIA files about our operatives, going on the run, and then exposing himself like that doesn't make sense. His party has spewed hatred and bullshit for years, but what are they after now, specifically? With only four hundred members, it's not like they could carry off a coup or anything. But the few bits of information we have lead us to believe he's got some kind of terrorist plan in the works. We have theories, but we can't put our finger on any one thing. He's not in any type of position to take real power, he doesn't run for office, nor has he inserted himself in politics. So, like Rowen said, there seems to be bigger things at play that we aren't seeing yet."

Jennifer was all too aware of the perplexing feeling they all felt, trying to put this puzzle together. What struck her in this moment was how personal Caden seemed to take it. Her face was pained, and Jennifer could tell she was trying to piece everything together in her head as she said the facts aloud. She seemed to carry the weight on her shoulders, which was ridiculous. Nonetheless, Jennifer appreciated her devotion. *Why have I never noticed this side of her before?*

CHAPTER TEN

B rooke stood at the vending machine. The choices were limited, and none of them were appealing. She wasn't hungry, but she needed a break.

"You should get the Reese's. They always make you feel better."

Brooke pushed the numeric combination and watched her favorite candy drop to the bottom of the machine. She reached in to get it before answering. "I don't think it'll do the trick this time."

"Must be serious."

Tyler never pushed her to talk before she was ready. She understood that Brooke often needed time to process a situation before divulging. But Brooke didn't want to talk. All she wanted to do was crawl into bed and lie in Tyler's arms until the pain went away. Or at least subsided. She also knew she *should* talk about it, since it would affect Tyler, whether she wanted it to or not. She hated to take any part in causing Tyler pain, and this situation with her parents was going to do just that.

"Lunch didn't go well."

Tyler stood next to her. She didn't touch her. She wouldn't within these halls, but her proximity was comforting. "They love you."

Brooke scoffed. She shouldn't have. Tyler was being supportive, and she didn't know what had unfolded. "I'm not so sure about that."

"They need time."

"I'm not sure time will fix this. They need a different daughter."

Tyler stood a bit closer. "They couldn't ask for a better daughter. I don't know what happened, but I do know that. They'll come around. They're your parents."

Brooke gritted her teeth. She desperately needed to keep from crying. "I don't think that's a job they want anymore. My mother made that clear. She's not your aunt Claire. I know that's hard for you to see, or even understand, but her love isn't unconditional. It's based on reputation and perspective. She isn't proud of this aspect of my life, and because she thinks it's a reflection on her, she'll try to make it go away."

"Brooke, I know it might seem like all hope is lost right now, but it's not. I truly believe your parents will come around. I have to believe that."

"Tyler, you have no idea what she's capable of once she sets her mind to something. This goes beyond just being disappointed in me, she could make life hard on you, too. Her reach is endless. You truly wouldn't even be able to imagine."

Tyler said nothing. The dark smudges under her eyes read of concern and exhaustion. Brooke realized right away she shouldn't have said anything. Tyler didn't need this, any of this, and Brooke was making it worse by further explaining the lengths her mother would go to in order to prove a point. Brooke was trying to find the words to reassure her, to let her know it didn't matter how deeply her mother dug her heels in, that it wouldn't affect her feelings. She was just about to tell her as much when Tyler smiled at her, breathed in deeply, and gave her an extended blink, which was their silent signal at work for, "I love you."

Brooke appreciated what Tyler was trying to do for her. Tyler was being Tyler. She was understanding, thoughtful, and compassionate. Tyler, despite all of the tragedy and pain that she witnessed, still believed that people were good and that families had the best of intentions. It was one of the things that Brooke loved about her. It was also where they differed.

Brooke's parents had never showered her or any of her brothers with love and affection. Yes, they supported them financially and wanted them all to have good lives. But Brooke never felt as if their love was unconditional. Not the way Claire loved Tyler. Brooke needed to excel in every aspect of her life, and even when she did that, her parents always thought she could do more. She never really felt as if she were good enough in their eyes and often found herself wondering if they were proud of her at all. All of their accolades seemed to be followed with a "but." Their home was lined with trophies, certificates, achievements, and honors. However, family pictures were scarce. She spoke with them once a week, but Brooke felt as if even those phone calls were progress reports, her parents checking up on her more than checking in. And in Brooke's mind, there was a difference.

She went back toward the control center, eating her candy. Tyler silently beside her, her support, as always, steady and un-wavering. She checked her phone, on the off chance that Tyler was right and her parents would change their minds. The plain screen indicated they hadn't. *It doesn't matter*. She had work to do. They all did. She wasn't going to let them distract her from this. Lark needed to be stopped, and it was going to be them that did it.

She needed normalcy. "What's your take on Rowen Knight?"

Tyler always let her change the conversation when she needed to. "I think we need to keep an eye on her."

"Oh?"

"Yes. In my experience, people don't often fall into your lap that can help you the way she says she can."

"I fell into your lap." Tyler smiled. Brooke loved her smile, and it was exactly what she needed to see right now.

"Yes, and I believe I tried to keep you at bay."

"Ha! You didn't try all that hard."

Tyler winked at her. "You're very stubborn. You wouldn't take no for an answer."

"I usually get what I want."

"You don't have to tell me that."

They had reached the control room. Brooke was happy she'd had these few minutes with Tyler. It helped her refocus.

"You're lucky I'm so stubborn. If I'd left it all up to you, we wouldn't be together."

"I would've figured it out. Eventually."

Brooke fought the urge to touch her. "That's what you tell me."

Tyler stopped her at the door. "In all seriousness, we *are* missing something. Rowen had no reason to be captured. She could have walked into CIA headquarters, identified herself, and we could have gone from there. She's playing some kind of game, and we need to figure out what the game is before we become pawns in it."

Tyler's intuition was usually spot-on in situations like this. "What do you need me to do?"

Tyler put her hands on her hips and stared at the wall behind Brooke for a moment. "Dig deeper. Find out what we're missing. I seriously doubt her government turned over all the information we have on her."

"I can do that. I'll need Jen's help."

"Good, thank you."

Tyler pulled the door open, and Brooke followed. It hadn't been much time together, but it was enough to rejuvenate Brooke and reassure her. Both personally and professionally, they were a team, and Brooke couldn't think of anyone she would rather be teamed up with.

❖

"If you can't do it, you need to say as much."

Rowen's voice was the first thing Tyler heard as she came through the door. Her time with Brooke had been brief but needed. Reality hit her in the face once she was back inside the room.

"I didn't say I couldn't do it. I just said it was going to take me a while."

Jennifer was frustrated, and it showed in her expression. Caden was sitting at a table several feet back from them, watching their conversation.

"I don't understand what *a while* means." Rowen crossed her arms.

Tyler interjected. "Knight, Glass is the best at what she does. If she said it's going to take her a while, I assure you, there is no one who could get it done faster. So back off."

Brooke sat down next to her. "What are we doing? Let me help."

Jennifer focused on Brooke. "Our very friendly French agent here gave me a *possible* location for the mainframe. I'm scanning the area, looking for bouncing IP addresses."

Brooke finished her thought. "Because if you can find a bouncing IP location, we might have our system. And Lark will be nearby."

"Yes. I know we're assuming the mainframe itself is in the camp, but that doesn't really matter when we're trying to access it from a specific IP address. It's a good starting location, but the signal bounces every four seconds, making it difficult to grab and truly pin down."

Caden interjected. "What can we do to help?"

Jennifer didn't look up, nor did her typing slow. "You can go do something else while we work. We'll let you know as soon as we have something."

Caden didn't seem to like this response. "Just twiddle our thumbs?"

"Special Agent Styles, I don't care what you twiddle, as long as it's not in here."

Tyler noticed the additional anger that seemed to be woven into Jennifer's words. She was upset with Caden, and Tyler didn't fully understand why. She knew they had a strained relationship at times, but there was definitely an undercurrent between them now.

"Come on, Styles. Let's get Knight situated and let them do their job. When it's our turn, they'll let us know."

"I'm not going anywhere." Rowen Knight was apparently just as stubborn as everyone in the room, which was counterproductive.

Rezentes came from his corner, seeming pleased by the palpable tension. "We could go grab something to eat. I haven't been to France in years, but I enjoyed my time there. Perhaps you could give me some ideas on where I should visit next."

Tyler saw Rowen roll her eyes, and for a moment, liked her just a little bit more.

"Fine. I'll go with you two." She pointed at Tyler and Caden.

Rezentes stalked back over to his corner with his proverbial tail between his legs. Tyler wondered for maybe the six-hundredth time what purpose he served.

Tyler caught Brooke's eye before she left the room, giving her what she hoped Brooke realized was a reassuring smile. Brooke was Tyler's calm space, and with everything being so messy right now, she needed these little moments. Tyler didn't know what was going on with Brooke's parents, or where Rowen was leading them, if anywhere helpful. She wasn't sure what weird dynamic was taking place between Caden and Jennifer. But what she did know was Brooke calmed her. She needed that calm right now. She needed a clear head to keep moving forward to complete the circle with Lark.

CHAPTER ELEVEN

Tyler walked with Rowen and Caden to one of the fleet SUVs. Caden climbed into the front seat next to her, and Rowen got in the back. She fastened her seat belt and caught Tyler's eye in the rearview mirror. "You always drive?"

Tyler wasn't sure why it was important. "Usually, why?"

Rowen looked out the window. "I figured. You're just the type. You seem like a bit of a control freak."

Tyler glanced over at Caden, who smirked. "I'm not a control freak."

Caden smiled at her. "You are, a little bit."

"You don't even like to drive."

Caden glanced over her shoulder. "That's also true."

Rowen continued to stare out the window. "How long have you two been together?"

Caden chuckled and pointed between herself and Tyler. "We are *not* together."

Rowen turned toward the front of the car, no amusement in her expression. "I meant as partners, you know, like working together."

Caden opened her mouth to answer, and Tyler cut her off. "Why does that matter?"

The side of Rowen's mouth twitched, trying to hide a smile. "It was just a question."

"How long have you been with French Intelligence?" Tyler could play her little game too.

"Check my file."

Tyler watched her from the mirror. Rowen checked her watch and then made eye contact.

"Just take me to the bus station." Rowen put on her seat belt. "I have emergency clothes and other things there. Speaking of, what did you do with the clothes I was wearing when you brought me in?"

"We sent them through uniformed laundry. You can probably get them back now though," Caden said.

Tyler maneuvered the car down the streets toward the bus station. Rowen had presumably purchased a locker at the station and was keeping her supplies there, which she couldn't have brought to Lark's camp.

"How did you get them to trust you?" To Tyler's surprise, she answered without any hesitation.

"Terrorist organizations aren't all that picky when they find someone who wants to join. People imagine it impossible to buy into all their rhetoric, but many are quite convincing. That's what makes them so dangerous. They all believe in what they're doing. If you support their cause, they welcome you. If they do any checking, it's minimal, and I passed through that part easily." She paused for a moment before she continued. "That, and I can hit a target from a thousand yards."

"Bullshit," Caden said.

Rowen smiled at Caden's response. "I can, and I have. Anyway, they started by giving me menial tasks. I assume it was to prove my loyalty and to probably run a background check of some kind. Before long, I was given more responsibility."

Tyler focused on her again. "Well, they'll either think you died or that we have you in custody."

"Yes. Which would you prefer?"

"Death isn't beneficial. If this computer angle doesn't work out, we're going to need you to go back in."

Caden turned around in her seat. "If they think we captured you, they might think we turned you."

Rowen smiled. "Then I will convince them otherwise. I lie for a living, you know."

Caden turned back around, and Tyler wasn't sure if she liked her response or was considering other implications.

They pulled up to the bus station a few minutes later, and Caden turned back in her seat. "Give me the key, and I'll go get your stuff."

"I'll go."

Caden smiled. "No. After all, you already admitted to lying for a living. We're not going to take a chance on you taking off."

"Twelve C. Four, fourteen, ten. It's a combination. I don't like to carry anything that can be traced."

Caden hopped out of the vehicle and disappeared into the station.

"Why those numbers?" Tyler asked.

Rowen looked out the window. "Are we sharing now?"

"Just curiosity."

Rowen stayed silent. Tyler wasn't going to cut her any slack, but getting information out of her was proving to be a trying process.

"Look in my file."

"If we're going to work together, you're going to need to start answering questions with a little more detail." Tyler picked up her phone from the middle console and checked the screen. Still no news from Brooke. No news about Rowen, no news about how she was feeling. Tyler put the phone back down and tried to fight off the worrisome feeling in her belly that thrummed with concern for Brooke.

"Wife checking on you?"

"Are we sharing now?"

Rowen smiled. "Touché."

Two could play this game, but the smile might be something of an opening. Tyler decided to take the topic off Rowen's private life and focus on another topic she might be willing to talk about. "Why is France interested in Lark?"

The answer was an obvious one, but Tyler wanted to see if Rowen would tell the truth. More so, she wanted to begin to learn what Rowen looked like when she was telling the truth, so she'd have a baseline to work with.

"Right now, Lark is the most interesting man in the entire world. He managed to not only deceive one aspect of your government, but several. That ability is a dangerous one. The National Front has a growing stronghold in the French government, and we're interested in any and all like-minded people. Lark is one of those people. We have reason to believe he's working with our own neo-Nazi party in France, and we want to know how far his reach goes."

"Why didn't your government just contact us? We could have worked together from the start."

Rowen let out a small laugh. "Would you have accepted help from us if it was offered?"

"That wouldn't have been my call to make. I follow orders."

Rowen made eye contact now. "You wouldn't have."

"You don't know that."

Rowen sighed loudly. "I do know that. America doesn't like to admit needing help from anyone. You only accept it in the direst of circumstances, and even then, it is begrudging."

"You seem to be speaking from personal experience."

"No. I've simply picked up a newspaper or two in my life."

Tyler would have given almost anything to have the gift of mind reading in this moment. Rowen's expression was calm, giving nothing away, but she was clearly deep in thought. "It seems our objectives are in line then. We all want to apprehend Lark." It was only partially true. She still had no idea what Rowen was after, but she did know she wasn't getting the full story.

Rowen ran her knuckles across her chin. "So it seems."

Caden opened the car door and hopped inside. She tossed the two bags into the backseat. "I thought for sure you would have a big ass gun in there."

"I do." Rowen pulled the bags up on her lap and started to unzip one.

"Bullshit."

Rowen tilted the bag forward so Caden could see. She pulled aside the clothes, revealing a hidden pocket at the bottom. She unzipped it and showed it to them.

"Jesus. That must be in like six pieces."

"Nine. And I can assemble it in under fifteen seconds."

"I'd ask you to prove it, but I believe you for some reason." She hit Tyler in the shoulder. "She might even give you a run for your money."

Tyler glared at Caden for the punch, then retrained her eyes on Rowen through the rearview mirror. "Maybe." She paused. "Look, Knight, I need a straight-up answer from you, no more dancing around the subject. If we're supposed to trust you, I need you to be honest. Why did you let us capture you? Why did you want to come in?"

Rowen stared back at her in the mirror, but the look in her eyes was unreadable. Then, her eyes changed, seemingly resigned to answering the question. "I've been with Lark's men for quite some time, but they have no idea I'm French Intelligence. The only way I could come in and get your help was to be captured. Being captured keeps my cover in check with them while still having access to all of you and what you know."

Tyler was annoyed, but a part of her believed what she was saying. "Why didn't you just say that?"

"I needed to know I could trust you. I don't know how far Lark's reach goes, but it's further than any of us can imagine."

"Okay, but you still have been intentionally obtuse."

"Yes."

Tyler was trying to push the annoyance down since she was making headway. "Why?"

"Because if I reveal everything, I have no bargaining position. I came in outnumbered, unsure of your credibility, and I don't enjoy giving up the upper hand."

"So, it's a mind game?"

"Call it whatever you want. I'm being honest with you now."

"Are you?"

"I guess you'll just have to roll the dice and trust me."

"We'll see."

Tyler didn't like games. Under other circumstances, she would have refused to work with Knight. But they needed her, and Rowen was right. She was going to have to roll the dice.

❖

"Easy now."

Brooke and Jennifer had been pounding away at the computer system for almost six hours. They had found a series of conspicuous firewalls, and now they were in the process of poking at them, trying to find their weak spots. Jennifer was convinced this was the mainframe they had been trying to isolate.

"There has to be a back door," Brooke said.

"There always is."

A moment later, Brooke said, "I think I may have found it."

Jennifer slid her chair over to Brooke's station. She watched her hammer away on the keyboard. The code was impressive, almost beautiful. She didn't want to jinx it, so she let her work without interruption.

Rezentes stood behind them. His labored breathing was starting to shred Jennifer's limited tolerance for him. "It's about time you two made some progress."

Neither acknowledged him. Jennifer pointed to the screen instead. The exhilaration of closing in on their goal was sending pinpricks of excitement throughout her body. This was one of the reasons she went into this line of work, the chase. She'd had her choice of professions when she completed college, but the CIA had appealed to not only her sense of patriotism but the ability to make a difference, and they were on the verge of making a massive one with this mission.

"There it is. Good job," she said to Brooke.

"I'm going to slip the rootkit in and get out before we're detected. These firewalls are everywhere."

Jennifer couldn't move or speak. This was a delicate process, and any misstep in a key stroke could alert the custodians of the program to their presence, something they couldn't afford. A few moments later, Brooke made a few loud keystrokes and then fell back into her seat, her arms falling over the sides of the chair. "That was intense."

Jennifer patted her back. "That was awesome. If it worked, we should have viable intel within the next day or so."

Rezentes pulled out his phone. "I need to let the director know."

"I thought we were supposed to keep this quiet from as many people as possible. We aren't even sure if it worked yet." Rezentes made a grunting noise. *He would have made a fabulous gorilla. If he smelled better.* Jennifer glanced at Brooke, who rolled her eyes.

"Analyst Glass, you worry about your job, and I'll worry about mine." His voice faded as he left the room, already talking to someone on the phone.

Brooke squeezed Jennifer's hand. "I'm going to call Monroe, Styles, and Knight. We need to start putting together our next move. We don't know how long we can monitor the messages without being detected. I've never seen a system with so much security. There's not even a way to tell how many sweeps or custodial components are present."

Jennifer didn't say anything. Brooke was right, their time was limited, but the thought of seeing Caden and Rowen was about as appealing as gouging out her own eye.

Brooke wasn't stupid and didn't let Jennifer's silence slide this time. "What is your deal anyway? I know you and Caden annoy each other, but it seems to have gotten worse."

Jennifer wanted to tell her. There was no reason she shouldn't tell her. Brooke was her friend, and she did want to talk to someone about what she was feeling, as foreign as that particular desire was. *Don't be a coward.* "Did I ever tell you about the night I slept with Caden?" She stared up at the ceiling because she didn't want to see Brooke's reaction.

"You mean, you fell asleep at Caden's one night for some reason, and she happened to be next to you. Right?"

Jennifer continued to stare at the speckled ceiling tiles, pointlessly hoping they would open up and swallow her whole. "No. I mean I had sex with Caden."

The machines around them hummed and clicked, filling the silence. Then Brooke said, "Tell me everything."

Jennifer did as she was asked. She went through the whole night over again. To Brooke's credit, she only stopped her to ask reasonable questions. She never asked anything about her sexuality or probed her on why Caden was the only woman she had ever heard about her being with.

"That explains so much."

"Does it? Because I feel like the only thing it has left me with is a million more questions and feeling like I'm always a little out of place. I have all of these thoughts and emotions that bounce around inside me, and I'm scared the only one who can settle them is Caden, who isn't an option."

"Well, why didn't you give her a chance?"

Jennifer ticked the reasons off on her fingers. "Because she's a child in about a million different ways. Because she's incapable of true intimacy, and because there's always a line of about ten women who want to pull her into bed. I don't need that kind of drama."

"So, you're scared."

"I'm not scared. I calculated the risks versus reward and decided that this was the only perceivable outcome. When you get involved with someone like Caden, there's only one way something like that ends."

"That's ridiculous. You have no idea how it would've turned out."

Jennifer laughed, though it was half-hearted. "Brooke, I love you, but not everyone is you and Tyler. Some things are never meant to be, no matter how appealing they are in a passing moment."

"But—"

"But what? She's arrogant, selfish, and a total player."

"But—"

"I mean, she has her good points too. She's a good listener, she's funny, and she's not painful to look at."

"And…"

Jennifer pushed Brooke's chair away from her own. "And I like her." Jennifer had never admitted out loud that she had feelings for Caden, worried that saying them would give them life, give them control over her. Jennifer believed in science, in rational, measurable outcomes. Having feelings for Caden didn't line up in any of those scenarios. Falling for Caden was like signing a death decree for her heart. *Okay, maybe that was a little dramatic.* Dramatic yes, but inaccurate? Caden was only interested in her because she couldn't have her, she liked the chase, and Jennifer didn't want to be prey. *Women who look like Caden Styles don't end up with girls that look like me.*

She glanced over at Brooke, who was talking on the phone. She had one arm crossed across her chest, exposing her toned biceps. *People like Caden fall for people like Brooke.* Jennifer pushed at the soft tissue that hung at her triceps. *Ugh!* She knew that if she gave herself over to what she was thinking, what she was feeling, all that would remain after being ravished by the storm that was Caden Styles would be a million fragments of what used to be her heart. Caden had the potential to obliterate her and she knew it. She'd known it the first time she kissed her, and there was no mistaking the damage Caden would inevitably unleash on her heart.

❖

Caden was listening. She *should* have been listening, anyway. Anyone looking at her would assume she was engulfed in what Brooke was saying at the front of the room. She heard words like "rootkit" and "administrative access." But what she was focused on was the way Jennifer was looking at her. Her eyes shimmered with anger and annoyance, and it looked like those emotions were directed right at her. The worst part was she had no idea what she did wrong. She never really did when it came to Jennifer. She seemed to be in a constant state of annoyance with her. *Except for the night she was in my bed.*

"Let me put it another way. A rootkit is a shield of sorts. Its job is to hide the fact that we have placed a virus in their system. The virus won't shut down their system, nor will it incapacitate it. This virus is letting us watch the messages that are being sent back and forth. Rootkits aren't foolproof, though. If the custodians of the program are paying close attention, which we assume they are, they'll find it sooner or later. We're just hoping for later. In the meantime, we need to take advantage of whatever information we can gain from the information that will flow through the rootkit."

Rowen stretched, her tight T-shirt pulling taut over her flat stomach. She looked almost bored. "I can make contact with the organization again, so when it gets reported through the messaging system, we will be able to see how it works and who is receiving the messages."

Brooke leaned over, putting both hands on the desk. "That's exactly what we had in mind."

"It could be dangerous. If you're made, we won't be able to get to you before they kill you for being a snitch." Tyler usually worked in worst-case scenarios when it came to missions, which was helpful.

Jennifer shrugged. "Well, none of us can go with her to meet the contact. Lark knows who each of us are, so we have to assume they're all aware. We could always send in someone else from your team."

Rowen leaned her head against her fist, her elbow leaning on the desk. "Bringing anyone else to a meet-up would be more dangerous. It wouldn't be like me to suddenly have a sidekick, and no one else knows the group well enough to infiltrate now."

Caden watched all of the interactions. Tensions were running high, but for a good reason. They were making progress, and this was the closest they'd ever been to not only apprehending Lark, but getting crucial evidence to use against him at trial. "Rowen knows what she's doing. I say we let her go back undercover." If Rowen was able to execute their plan, it would prove she could be trusted, which would help to ease everyone's mind. She didn't necessarily like the idea of Rowen being in harm's way, but this was how missions worked. And if Rowen was working for Lark, if she had turned, they still had a shit ton more information than they had when she first arrived.

Rowen smiled at her. It was an appreciative smile, a silent thank-you of sorts. "I think it's our best shot."

The door beeped, and Deputy Director Martin appeared, with Rezentes trailing behind. He looked around and took a seat at the table, Rezentes mirroring his movements. "I heard we've made some progress. I'm caught up thus far. Please, continue."

Brooke motioned to Rowen. "You've spent the most time inside the organization. What are your thoughts?"

Rowen pushed her cell phone forward on the table. She had already explained to Caden and Tyler that this was her way of communication with Lark's group. Lark's crew had placed a tracking device inside it to be able to keep tabs on her, but she'd discovered the device and rewired it, so it would transmit her location wherever she told it to. "All I have to do is call in."

"And say what, exactly?" Rezentes's tone was accusatory. Apparently, he hadn't liked her turning down his company in favor of Tyler's and Caden's after all.

"I'll tell them that I want to come back. Tell them that I was able to get some information out of one of the agents, and that

I'm still stringing her along. Tell them I'm playing both sides, for their benefit." Rowen looked at Caden and winked.

Caden unintentionally looked at Jennifer. Jennifer, with her aloof attitude and dismissive gaze. Jennifer, who she couldn't seem to get out of her mind since the night they had shared. Jennifer, who wanted nothing to do with her.

"Perfect." Deputy Director Martin slapped the desk. "We might be able to get our agent on the inside."

"Will they believe you?" Jennifer asked.

Rowen smiled at Caden. "Oh, they'll believe me. If I choose the right agent to play the part of the one I've been able to turn."

"You going to buy me dinner first?" Caden made the offhand comment to make light of the situation, but the look on Jennifer's face indicated that not everyone thought it was funny. She looked hurt. Caden wished she could take it back.

Rowen smiled. "Sure."

Martin started toward the door. "Special Agent Monroe, Special Agent Styles, I would like you both in my office tomorrow morning at zero nine hundred hours. I'd like to go over the details of the next stage of the operation, once you have them ironed out. And in case I'm not clear, I want them ironed out by tomorrow morning at zero nine hundred. I want to know exactly what we've been able to find out from the rootkit and the progress Knight has made with her old handler from Lark's organization. We need to know if they will bring her back into the fold, if they still trust her. If they do still trust her and are willing to work with her, we'll go from there."

Rezentes didn't bother to hide his contempt. "Fill me in too." He followed Martin from the room.

Tyler leaned forward on the table. She was looking at the screens filled with various codes, maps, documents, and pictures. Caden knew she wasn't looking at them for information, but she was thinking. "You should say that you turned me." She didn't look up when she said it, clearly working out the details in her head.

"You?" Rowen walked over to the computer screens. "I don't like the idea of having to bring anyone else in on this. Having too many people in the mix is when mistakes happen. But if you're going to insist, it needs to be Caden. Not you."

"You just expect us to trust you. How do we know you aren't leading Caden into some type of trap?"

Rowen shrugged. "You don't."

"But you're okay potentially endangering Caden? Just not me?" The anger in Tyler's voice was rising.

"I don't want Caden to be a part of anything, but I can't convince them that I'm playing both sides unless they believe I've actually turned one of you. Caden is the more believable of the two of you."

"It has to be me." Caden said it without thinking. "If they really do know about us, our habits, our interactions, I'm much more believable."

Rowen motioned in Caden's direction, indicating her agreement. "Even that won't be an easy sell, but it's worth a shot. Tyler, you exude hero cop out your pores. No one would believe you'd turn. But Caden?" Rowen's eyes traveled over Caden the way they had when they'd first brought her into the station. "She's more rogue cop than hero cop. Believable. I'll call them tonight and arrange a time where I can go meet with them. Caden, you'll need to come home with me. After I call in and allow them to really see my location, they could be watching me. It would be best if you were with me."

"For the mission's sake, right?" Jennifer crossed her arms and glared at Rowen.

Rowen smiled at her, a bit of mischief and challenge lurking in her expression. Caden hadn't spent much time with Rowen, but she knew enough to know that she could hide her emotions if she wanted or needed to. She also found it interesting that Jennifer sounded both protective and jealous. *She makes my frigging head spin. I wonder if she has any idea she's doing it?* She raised her eyebrow when Rowen looked at her with that same mischievous smile.

"Yes, for the mission." She looked back at Tyler. "Formulating a plan much beyond that, at this juncture, is pointless. I need to make sure they still trust me. We can go from there."

Brooke knelt in the chair, her forearms resting on the back ledge. "We can monitor any correspondence. They seem to send a lot of messages, most of which seem meaningless and intended to distract anyone who might be watching. Literally thousands are processed every few minutes. My best guess would be that they're acting as a text messaging service, which is the perfect cover. But I have an alert tacked on for keywords."

Rowen walked toward the door. She stopped and turned around. "Come on, Caden. We have work to do." She gave her a seductive wink.

Caden glanced at Jennifer on her way out the door. Her face was flushed red, but it could have been annoyance, anger, or a combination. Caden wasn't entirely sure what she had done to upset her, since she was just doing her job, playing a part they agreed she had to be the one to play. She wanted to pull her aside right then and there and demand she finally talk to her about what was going on. She wanted to make her talk about what she was feeling whenever she caught her looking in her direction, but now wasn't the time or the place. She had work to do and a mission to complete. Emotions, as always, would have to wait.

CHAPTER TWELVE

Tyler stared at Brooke from across their small kitchen table. She clung to the glass of wine as if it somehow helped to ground her. Her voice was broken, her words coated with the tears that slid down her face. Tyler's heart broke with each muted sob. She didn't understand how the two people that had helped to create the amazing woman in front of her could so carelessly and callously throw her away.

Brooke had managed to hold it together at work, which Tyler knew was a temporary escape. But now, in the quiet of their home, Brooke let her guard down. The pain had started bubbling to the surface on the drive home and finally spilled over when everything else was able to settle into the background.

Tyler wanted to say something, anything, that would take the pain away. She wanted to banish all the hurt and anger that Brooke was feeling. She also knew that wasn't possible. Brooke was going to need to find a way to cope, to recover, and to heal. Tyler rubbed her hands. She didn't know if she was angry, sad, or at a loss. This wasn't an enemy that hid in the darkest parts of their minds or in the shadows, waiting to pounce. These were her parents, and they had attacked, in full daylight, apparently with zero concern for casualties.

"I don't ever want to see them again." Brooke wiped the tears from her face. Then she took another sip of wine.

"Understandable. But maybe they'll come around." Tyler didn't know if it was true or not. She just couldn't imagine anyone wanting to remove themselves from Brooke's life.

"There're some words you can never take back."

"They just need time."

"Time? They need time?" Sadness was rapidly transitioning to anger. "I've been telling them the same thing for years. They've chosen to ignore it until they no longer had a choice."

Tyler nodded because she didn't know what to say. She wasn't going to be able to make this better. There were only two people that could do that, and she wasn't sure if that was going to happen. "Is there anything I can do?"

Brooke played with the cloth placemat that sat in front of her, pulling at the edges. "There's nothing to do. It is what it is."

Tyler knew it wasn't how Brooke really felt. Brooke had a habit of shutting down when she was hurt, and this was as hurt as she had ever seen her. She hoped her parents would come to their senses before it was too late. Brooke was as stubborn as they came, and damage was being done that could be irreparable if they waited too long.

"I'm going to take a bath." She grabbed the bottle of wine off the table and started toward their room.

"Okay, baby, let me know if you need anything."

Tyler heard the water turn on. She stared at her phone. It wasn't her place to call Brooke's parents, but then, it was her job to help Brooke as best as she could. She also knew she could do more harm than good. Brooke might be mad that she'd taken it upon herself to contact them, but what was the alternative? She could wait for them to come to their senses, but that didn't seem like a good idea either. If she didn't do something, and Brooke lost her parents forever, could she live with herself? *This relationship stuff is so damn complicated.* She unlocked Brooke's phone and copied the phone number into her own phone. She went out the front door, shutting it as quietly as possible behind her. She let her finger hover over the green button for a minute. She decided that even if Brooke was mad, she needed to help somehow.

The phone rang a few times. Tyler cursed herself for trying to get hold of them so late. Then a voice came on. "Hello?"

"Captain Hart?"

"Yes. Who is this?"

"Tyler Monroe. We need to talk, sir."

Jennifer maneuvered through the parking garage. It took her a moment to remember where she had last parked her car. Headquarters could play tricks on you, the same way a casino could. You could be ready to finally leave and not be totally sure if it was night, day, or how long you had been inside. She passed a nearly empty row of parking spaces when she heard a pair of voices talking in the distance. This wasn't abnormal. Everything in this garage echoed. You'd know people were talking, even if they were five hundred feet away.

But there was something off about these voices. It was as if they were trying to be quiet, and not succeeding. One of the voices she recognized as Rezentes. Jennifer had no idea what he was still doing at work and wondered who he could be berating now. Curiosity got the best of her. At the very least, it would make for a funny story to tell Brooke tomorrow.

She turned down the row to get a better look. His conversation counterpart was a very small woman Jennifer recognized. It was Speaker of the House Carol O'Brien. *What the hell?* Jennifer couldn't fathom why these two would need to have a conversation in a deserted parking lot late at night. There was only one way to find out, but she needed to get closer. She saw a cement pillar about thirty feet from where they were talking. Jennifer quickly and quietly slid behind the pillar unseen.

She closed her eyes and tried to remember the training she had received on the Farm. She knew that clandestine operations weren't her forte, but that wasn't going to stop her. She controlled her breathing and made sure not to peek around the large circular barrier, as much as she wanted to.

"I told you, I'll tell you as soon as I know something. You shouldn't have come here." Rezentes was angry. He was always angry, but this seemed to hold a different level altogether.

"I wouldn't have come if you had followed through on your end. You've had her in custody for over twenty-four hours."

"Yes, a busy twenty-four hours. I don't understand why you're so interested in her anyway."

"That isn't any of your concern. You're supposed to deliver information. Don't worry about why."

"I'm not just some dog you can command. I need to know what's happening." His voice was getting louder. Rezentes hated being told what to do, especially by women.

"No, but if you want a shot at a political career after your retirement, you need to do what is asked of you."

"You don't control everything. I'll get what I damn well deserve."

"That's your problem right there. You think everything is owed to you, that you're entitled to rewards for your time here. You're not, and if you think for one second that political careers aren't forged in parking lots just like this one, with plenty of other people, I apparently had you pegged wrong all along. Maybe you're not the man for the job after all, and I should approach one of the women on your team instead."

Jennifer was desperate to know what information she wanted from Rezentes. *Something big enough he thinks he'll get a big payoff from it.* She was so completely caught up in her curiosity that she peeked around the corner, forgetting her brief six-week training. She was instantly caught in Rezentes's line of sight.

He stiffened. "Shut up."

"You will not speak to me that way. Who the hell do you think pulls the strings in the White House right now—"

Jennifer pulled back behind the pillar, furious for having revealed herself. There was silence now, and Jennifer assumed that Rezentes was informing her that someone was listening. She looked around for a way out. *There's always a back door.* She decided the best back door was acknowledgment. She came around the corner.

"Evening! Sorry, I got so turned around looking for my car." She spoke too loudly, as though worried they wouldn't hear her from where she was.

They were coming toward her, quickly.

"I'm such a scatterbrain sometimes. I got myself all turned around. Have a good night."

She turned away from them and started in the opposite direction, mentally pleading for any type of divine intervention.

She heard the popping noise before she felt what she knew was coming. It sounded like a cap gun. In the split second before the barbs came into contact with her back, she knew what was about to happen. She lost complete control of her body, went entirely stiff, and fell to the ground. The paralysis was instant. Her body was quaking, and she could hear the snapping of the electricity. She knew that she was gritting her teeth. She knew her body was shaking. She was cognizant yet completely impaired. She was terrified.

Rezentes and Carol O'Brien stood over her. They were arguing about what had just taken place.

"What the hell is wrong with you?"

Rezentes pointed down at Jennifer's shaking body. "I assure you, this one would have been a liability."

"Well, she definitely is now. You're an idiot. Now I have to clean up your mess again." If Jennifer had been able to speak, she would have emphatically told them she wasn't going to be a liability, that she didn't need to be taken care of, in any way they were envisioning.

Swearing and breathing heavily, Rezentes carried her over to a plain black Honda Civic and threw her in the trunk. She was starting to get the feeling back in her body, and the scream that had been caught in the back of her throat, held hostage by thousands of volts of electricity, was getting ready to erupt. Then came the needle. O'Brien pulled it out of her jacket pocket and pushed it directly into her neck. The hope of managing a scream died, and the darkness came next. It was full, deep, and all consuming. The few seconds of consciousness that were afforded to her were a montage of missed moments. Moments she could have spent with Caden, moments she should have told her how she felt. Moments she wasn't going to be able to get back.

CHAPTER THIRTEEN

Caden attempted to take a mental inventory of the sparse, one-bedroom apartment. It didn't take long. There was nothing except the bare essentials. Not a single picture, a randomly placed personal item, nothing. She sat on the couch, still looking around, trying to piece together any bits of information she could gather about the elusive woman that stood ten feet away. She noted the flirtatious undertone that Rowen used when speaking with the person on the other end of the line as she made the phone call they were hinging their next steps on. Rowen used her sexuality as a weapon, lulling people into comfortable acceptance, though she was hatching her next move with each step. It was calculated, precise, and if Caden was being honest, impressive. Rowen seemed to understand how to work each and every person she came into contact with to get exactly what she needed. This was instinct. It wasn't something they would have taught at French Spy School. *Or whatever it's called over there.*

She could only hear one side of the conversation, but Caden thought she was doing an excellent job spinning her story. She was concise and didn't include too much detail she could trip up on later. She explained exactly what they had spoken about earlier, that she wanted to come in and that she'd been able to gather some valuable information, which she was now able to get pretty much on demand. She giggled here and there, probably to imply her innocence in the situation. After the person on the other end seemed satisfied, she hung up and shrugged at Caden, her demeanor changing back to the agent they'd been talking to at headquarters. The rapid switch was disconcerting.

Caden was going to comment on the flirtation but decided against it. Rowen knew what she was doing. It had taken her this far and seemed to be serving her well, even if it did make Caden uncomfortable.

Rowen pulled off her shirt, and her fair skin bore the reflection of the one light inside the space. "I'm going to take a shower. Order some takeout."

Caden forced herself not to stare at the way her muscles twitched with each change of movement. At any other time, with any other woman, she would have taken the removal of clothing as an invitation, a clear indication they wanted more. This wasn't the case with Rowen. Caden knew it was a way to control a situation and the people in it, and she wasn't interested in playing that game, no matter how hot she was.

Rowen disappeared into the bathroom, and Caden pulled out her phone. One of her favorite Chinese places was around the corner, and she called in the order. She listened to the water fall from the shower and unintentionally thought of Jennifer. The morning after the night they had spent together, Caden had stood in the shower for much longer than necessary. She'd watched the water slide off her body, knowing it was taking the remnants of Jennifer with it. She had thought for several days, maybe even weeks, how to erase that night from her life. It had been one of the best ones she could remember, and that acknowledgment alone was painful. Jennifer had run from her. She didn't know why she still let it bother her. Caden never entertained the idea of being with one person for a prolonged period of time. Once the shininess of new love wore off, all anyone was ever left with was pain, regret, and self-loathing. She didn't need that. No one did.

Jennifer had been right to run from her. Caden wasn't girl-friend material. *It's not like I'm someone you bring home to meet the parents.* She was selfish, career-driven, and suffered from easy boredom. Jennifer was smart. She could see Caden's baggage coming from a mile away. Of course, she had no other choice than to head in the opposite direction, as quickly as possible.

Caden was built for one-night stands, trivial affairs that held the promise of nothing more than a night or two. Thinking about it now, her attraction to Rowen was probably rooted in their similarities. They seemed to be built from the same crappy material, capable of surface interest and shallow affairs, nothing more.

Rowen was standing in front of her, with her hair a wet mess, wrapped in a towel. Caden didn't realize the shower had shut off. Rowen's features were striking. The lines of her neck and shoulders were alluring, intoxicating. Part of her red hair lay across her shoulders, and small droplets from the tips of her hair slid down her chest, crashing into the white towel. Caden continued to look. She noticed dozens of scars under closer scrutiny, and her stomach tightened. She had seen these same scars at headquarters but hadn't given them much thought, knowing that people in their profession often had similar, long lasting wounds. Up close, however, they seemed different. They didn't strike Caden as blemishes, or proof of hard fought battles. Each one of those healed marks was a shove toward the place Rowen was in now. Caden didn't know if they were from knives, car accidents, or intimate confrontations, but they each played a part in turning Rowen into the guarded person standing in front of her. Caden knew this because hers were the same.

Rowen took a step closer. She looked as if she wanted to say something. Caden didn't want to talk. She didn't want to know. Knowing would make Rowen real. If Rowen was real, Caden wouldn't be able to protect herself from her if need be. Luckily, the doorbell rang, saving her from impending doom.

Caden jumped up and headed to the door. Rowen walked back into her room. She paid the delivery boy and gave him a generous tip. She laid out the food on the small kitchen table, not bothering to look for plates. She started pulling open the lids and grabbed a pair of chopsticks.

Rowen left her bedroom wearing a pair of loose basketball shorts and a tight, black tank top. She opened the fridge and pulled out two bottles of beer, then handed Caden one. She sat down and mimicked Caden's motions, looking in each food box and grabbing a pair of chopsticks. She leaned back in her chair and balanced her weight against the table using her right leg, partially folding it up underneath her.

"What's next?" Caden asked in between bites.

"You go to your meeting tomorrow morning. Tell your boss they're allowing me to come in and everything is going as planned. We'll have a solid avenue to Lark before you know it." She chewed. "And I'll go meet up with my handler, start getting the information we need, and we'll go from there. As soon as I can, I'll have you come in and we can start trying to recon the primary outpost."

Caden stared at her. "We should have someone following you, from a distance at least."

Rowen shook her head. "I appreciate your chivalry, but I can take care of myself. I don't need any of your people giving me away or scaring them."

"It's not chivalry. It's common sense, and my people are highly trained."

Rowen laughed mockingly. "I'll take my chances."

"I'll call in and get you set up with a wire then."

Rowen dropped her knee and rested her arms on the table. She had stopped chewing and set her food container down. "Caden, I have survived in this world for a very long time. Partially because I've taken chances and partially because I haven't. You need to know when it's the right time to take those chances, and tomorrow isn't one of them. I need to assume that they're going to check me for a wire, to see if I'm being followed or watched. They need to trust me as they always have. Risking that would be both deadly and ludicrous."

Caden thought about it for a moment. She knew Rowen was right, but she didn't want her to be. She wasn't sure if she could fully trust her, but she didn't like the idea of her walking into something so blindly. It didn't sit right, but she also understood this wasn't an argument she was likely to win. "Fine."

Rowen resumed her relaxed position, leaning back and eating. The silence was comfortable, but Caden felt like they should be doing more, working to put plans in place, figuring out possibilities. "So what's your plan?"

Rowen grabbed a piece of chicken out of the container and popped it in her mouth. "I'll figure it out as it happens. Making plans usually marries you to a certain set of ideas, and if something goes wrong, you hesitate. I don't like to hesitate."

"How long have you been doing all of this?" She used her chopstick to make a haphazard circle in the air.

Rowen took a deep breath. "If you're referring to my interactions with Lark, about eleven months. If you're talking about my actual job, for so long I can't remember. I'm an only child, not married, and I never went to college."

Caden didn't say anything. She knew most of it was a lie. Well, not a lie necessarily, but a premeditated answer to avoid any other questions. Everything Rowen disclosed was in her file, which had already been given to them. She knew that. "Any kids?"

Rowen momentarily stopped chewing and pushed around some food in her container. "Do I strike you as someone who has a gaggle of kids hiding somewhere?"

That was defensive. "It was just a question."

"It was a stupid question."

But not one you answered. Caden was going to let the subject rest for now. In all reality, it was none of her business anyway.

However, that didn't mean she wouldn't keep it in the back of her mind for later use, if needed.

"Where're we going to meet up, after you make contact tomorrow?"

Rowen now chomped on a piece of broccoli, presumably considering Caden's question. "I'll find you."

Caden was starting to get frustrated. "Look, Knight, you don't run things around here. These answers aren't going to cut it. Where're we going to meet?"

"Believe it or not, I'm not purposely trying to be evasive. I don't know what's going to happen tomorrow or how long they're going to want me around. I'll text you as soon as I know anything. You need to chill out. Stress isn't good for your blood pressure."

"Are you concerned about my blood pressure?"

Rowen smiled now. "Not really. I just figured that was something people say."

"Your kindness is admirable."

Rowen set her food on the table. She ran her hand lightly up Caden's arm. The touch was surprisingly gentle, such a contrast from Rowen's normal abrasive approach. Caden watched her hand travel up her arm. In her mind, she told it to stop, but the words didn't make it out of her mouth.

"I know a good way to reduce blood pressure."

Caden's cheeks flushed hot. Her arm tingled, and she felt a jolt through her body. "No thanks, I already worked out today."

"You disappoint me, Styles."

"Sorry." Caden shrugged. She was attempting to seem aloof. She wasn't sure if it was working, but she was sure she had made her point. She wasn't sure why she had turned Rowen down so quickly. Falling into bed with her would have been easy and a welcome relief from the stress and intensity of the last few days. But despite her attraction, she just wasn't interested. Come to think of it, she hadn't really been interested in anyone since

Jennifer. That thought alone almost shoved her out of her seat and toward Rowen. Surely a night with her would be a good foot forward in banishing Jennifer from her memory.

Rowen got out of her seat, heading toward the bedroom. "If you change your mind, you know where I am." She pulled off her shirt as she turned the corner into the dark room.

Desire and curiosity embraced Caden. It squeezed her tightly, pushing a small noise from the back of her throat. Her body wanted to follow Rowen, to spend a few hours with careless abandon. She needed this. She went to follow Rowen but stopped in the hallway and pinched the bridge of her nose, trying to figure out what the hell she wanted. She considered the possible aftermath and made a right turn into the bathroom instead.

A few minutes later, she lay on the couch and closed her eyes. She hung her arm over the side, her fingertips tracing the outline of her gun that lay holstered beside her. She knew sleep wouldn't come easy, but it was a necessity. Images of Rowen, Jennifer, and Lark danced across her eyelids. They framed the terribly painted picture that was her current life. A life she couldn't completely make sense of, nor did she know where to begin. Lark was easy; he fit nice and neat into a large box that sat on her mental work shelf. Rowen and Jennifer, on the other hand, moved around her mind, penetrating different areas, never settling into one section or another.

She didn't know what game Rowen was playing, but she'd managed to capture her interest. Sure, they could spend a few hours together, maybe over the course of several weeks, and then it would be over. They both would have their needs met, and it would all be tied up in a pretty little box of closure. Simple, clean, and no hurt feelings. Unless, of course, it turned out she really was playing them all, and she screwed Caden by putting her in the line of fire. There was that, too.

Then there was Jennifer. Her every turn, every look, *everything,* was laced with underlying meaning and mixed messages.

She replayed the night with Jennifer all over again. The warm sensation that spread through her body whenever she thought about it engulfed her at once. She thought about Jennifer's hands on her, the intensity in her eyes, the way she bit her lip as she climaxed. Then, the look on her face when she woke up the next morning. The look of embarrassment in her eyes when she realized she was with Caden. Even now, she wasn't sure what she had been thinking or feeling. *You're such a coward.* She could've asked Jennifer to talk to her, or more likely, bugged her until she agreed. But did she really want to hear the answers to her questions? Did she really want to see herself through Jennifer's eyes? She assumed it wasn't a very pretty picture. The thought made her stomach and chest hurt. One thing was certain, she wasn't good enough for someone like Jen. She was smart, funny, and ambitious. Caden was used to sleeping with beautiful women, but they never ranked very high in other areas. No, pursuing Jennifer would only lead to rejection and heartbreak. So it should be easy to let the whole thing go and move on.

Sure, easy.

CHAPTER FOURTEEN

Tyler was nervous. Brooke knew all the signs. She paced back and forth in their apartment. She had already been out for her run, which typically would have left her calm and together, but that wasn't the Tyler she was dealing with. Brooke sipped her coffee and glanced at the clock. There was still two hours before she had her meeting with Martin. It couldn't be that, Tyler didn't worry about things like that. It had to be something else.

"Something bothering you?"

Tyler stopped her pacing and looked over at her, her eyes full of worry, her brow furrowed. She put her hand over her mouth and looked down at the ground. "I did something, and I think you are going to be very mad at me."

Brooke laughed. "I seriously doubt that. Come over here and talk to me. What happened?"

There was a knock on the door. Brooke's stomach dropped. A knock at this hour usually meant something happened. Something bad, to someone they cared about. She put down her coffee cup as Tyler approached the door. She looked at Brooke before opening it, giving her an apologetic smile.

Her father arrived a few moments later. Anger, surprise, and betrayal surged through Brooke's body. Her fingertips felt like they were on fire, her body rigid. She felt like a child all over again, preparing for a reprimand. But in this instance, it was a reprimand she didn't deserve and had no intention of entertaining.

Tyler walked over to Brooke, standing between her and the man that she shared a blood type with. The man who had carried her in his arms to the hospital when she was nine and had a fever so severe she needed the emergency room. The man who had teared up at her high school and college graduations. The man who had disowned her.

Brooke looked past Tyler; she would deal with her later. He stood there looking the most casual she could remember seeing him. He wore dark blue jeans with a United States Navy sweatshirt and held a baseball cap in his hands. "What are you doing here?" The sound of her own voice surprised her. It was husky and deep, as if her vocal cords had been dragged across sandpaper.

"I'd like to talk to you."

"I think you said everything you needed to yesterday." She crossed her arms, not wanting her hands to shake. "Or more accurately, Mom said everything and you agreed."

"Brooke, honey, please try to understand—"

"There is nothing to understand." She waved away his words. "You made it pretty clear how you feel about me, about Tyler, about my life."

"I don't expect you to understand. You aren't a parent. But you have these ideas about what your children will grow up to be. These expectations—"

"Yes, Dad, I know. I don't meet your expectations. You wanted me to grow up, marry a man, and have children. You wanted me to work in the corporate world. You wanted all these things for me that I never had any interest in. You don't listen to me. You've never listened to me."

"When did you start talking to me like this?"

Brooke's chest hurt. The pressure was constricting her breathing, his words squeezing her heart to the point she thought it might just pop like a balloon, leaving her empty. "Dad, I think this is the first real conversation we've ever had. A real conversation means both people speaking, not one person speaking while the other passively listens."

She watched him. He fidgeted with his hat, clearly unsure what to say next. She had never seen him like this. He looked a bit defeated, like he had given up, or wanted to.

Finally, he said softly, "Okay, then please explain it to me."

This was the last thing Brooke expected to hear from her father. She had expected more of the same ignorance, blind ridicule, maybe, but not understanding. It took her a moment to gather her composure. "I love her." Her body was starting to catch up with the mental realization she had just made, and tears formed in her eyes. "I love her more than I have ever loved anyone or anything. It's not going to change, not for Mom, or you, or anyone. She is my life now, a life I want you and Mom to be a part of, but only if you understand that."

He stared at Tyler for what seemed like hours. To her credit, Tyler didn't flinch under his scrutiny. Brooke wasn't sure what he was thinking, but there was no anger in his eyes.

"Where do you stand on all of this?" he asked Tyler.

Tyler straightened. "Sir, I will be here for as long as Brooke allows it. It'd be the greatest privilege of my life."

He took a deep breath and ran his hand through his hair. "You know, as a parent, you wait your whole life to hear someone worthy talk about one of your children that way. I don't know if you are worthy yet, but I'm willing to give you a chance."

Brooke had her arms wrapped around him before he could finish his sentence. He was surprised at first, but his arms were around her moments later. The embrace was hesitant, but then became a warm, tight blanket around her. She felt the tears running down her cheeks, hot and salty. "Thank you, Dad."

His face had become flushed, and his eyes were red and tearing. "I want you to be happy, sweetie. I may be old, but I'm not blind. I can see what you two feel for each other."

Tyler put her hand on her shoulder and squeezed.

"But I can't make any promises about your mother. I'll try and talk to her, but it might take her a while."

Brooke wanted to interject and say how ridiculous that was, how her mother should accept her exactly the way she was, but her father put his hand up to stop her words before they came out.

"Give her some time, Brooke, please."

"Okay, Dad."

He turned toward the door. "I'll let you two go. I know how much you have going on at work."

"I'll call you soon."

He pulled the door open and smiled at her. "I hope so, honey. Remember that I love you. Bye, Tyler."

"Have a good day, sir."

The door shut and Brooke stood there for a moment, a bit in shock. Tyler picked her up and kissed her cheek. "I told you everything would be all right."

Brooke was enjoying the small victory. It was unexpected and appreciated, but this wasn't over. Her mother wouldn't go down without a fight, and Brooke knew it would be a long, fifteen-round fight. But Tyler was right. This was a big step, and her father's acceptance was important to her. She would appreciate the small victories when they happened because you never knew how long it would be until your next one.

CHAPTER FIFTEEN

Jennifer willed her eyes to open. Her brain was groggy, mushy. She was focusing on telling her arm to lift. When that didn't work, she tried her hand, then finger. Nothing. It was like being caught in the in-between, where dreams and reality meet. The sensation of wanting to wake yourself up and not being able to complete the menial task. Your brain misfiring information, because what other reason could there be, when you were so clearly focused on completing an action that was taken for granted millions of times before.

The door opened. Voices. Not voices she recognized, which was disconcerting for a number of reasons. Then a set of hands were on her face, pulling her eyelids open. White light flashed back and forth. She knew they were checking for dilation, brain activity. *Great.* She momentarily thought she might be in a hospital room. Those hopes were dashed when the images started coming back to her. It was like watching a B-rated horror flick. Rezentes and Carol O'Brien, the bolt of electricity, the car, and then that needle. It'd been stupid to try to eavesdrop. Stupid to think that she could get away with it. She wasn't built like Caden and Tyler. She was built for computers, ciphering information out of places that no one else could get to. Not this.

Her hand twitched. *Finally.* A few moments later, she could feel her arm, and then feeling spread to the rest of her body. Then the pain rushed through her, and everything hurt. There wasn't a single spot on her body that wasn't thrumming, feeling as if she had been hit by a truck. She must have hit the ground hard. She didn't think anything was broken, because despite the seering pain, nothing was protruding and she was able to wiggle her appendages. She was sure she could move each limb if need be. She opened her eyes. A man was pulling a needle out of an IV hooked up to her hand.

"Where am I?"

He continued to jot on the clipboard he held, never even bothering to look at her. "Someone will be in to talk to you shortly."

He left without saying another word. She placed her hands on either side of her and tried to heave her bodyweight upright, barely sliding an inch. The small motion itself was exhausting. She felt depleted and confused. That feeling was rapidly replaced with a scorching thirst. She glanced at the table to her left. There was a small pitcher and a plastic cup sitting next to it.

She made the decision that she was going to use all her will, all her brainpower, to grab that pitcher from the table. To hell with the cup, she was going to drink the entire container. Her arm had made it halfway to the table when the door opened, startling her. She fell back against the bed, more out of surprise than fear.

"Ms. Glass, please don't be alarmed. We intend you no harm."

The man was shorter than his voice suggested he'd be. It was commanding, vibrant, and sincere. She continued to look him over. His build was average, dark hair, dark eyes. Caden and Tyler could take him out with one hit. This realization helped to put her at ease. "So what do you intend for me?"

He smiled, taking a seat on the corner of the bed. "That depends on you."

Maybe it was because her body thrummed with pain from the fall and the electricity. Maybe it was because whatever they had injected her with to knock her out was still in her system. Or maybe it was because she was tired and didn't want to participate in mind games that she wanted him to cut through his polite bullshit and get to the point. "Look, I was hammered with fifty-thousand volts of electricity, injected with some type of tranquilizer, and then thrown in the back of a car. I'm sorry if I don't feel like playing a cat-and-mouse game with you right now. So please, just tell me what you want."

He smiled, but this one wasn't genuine; it never reached his eyes. *People who smile without using their eyes are trying to manipulate or appease.* Either way, it wasn't for her benefit.

"We would like to give you the opportunity to join us."

She laughed. It hurt, but there was no other suitable reaction. This guy was clearly delusional. "You obviously know who I am and where I work. Who are you? What is the organization? What is it you'd think I'd do for you? What on earth makes you think that I would ever entertain the idea of becoming part of an organization that clearly had a hand in landing me here? Because right now, I assume that you're all involved in some pretty illegal shit."

He stood and ran his hands down his pants, undoing the small creases created when he sat down. "So many questions, but for now, I will only answer one. The answer to why you will help us is simple. Because if you don't, we'll kill your little sister." He motioned to a woman standing in the corner. Jennifer hadn't even noticed her. She handed him a plain manila folder. He opened it and started tossing pictures on her lap.

Jennifer's breath caught in her chest. Her sister was in the center of each shot, in various poses of her everyday life. At the coffee shop with her friends, walking out of the library, going to her car, kissing her boyfriend, leaving work, leaving class. She picked up each one, her hands trembling. She felt her eyes fill with tears and then blinked several times, attempting to fight them back. She needed to focus. She needed to regain control. She needed to be someone else.

"She's only twenty years old. Don't you people have any respect for human life?"

"We do, but only the lives we feel are worthy of that respect. White lives. Christian lives. Lives that can help us with our cause. Unfortunately for you, your sister doesn't currently fall into that category." He patted her leg like they were old friends, chatting, catching up. "I'll give you some time to think about your options. But not too long. I don't like to be kept waiting."

"Who are you?" She looked up at him, still gripping one of the pictures, her head pounding with anger and fear. She already knew the answer, it had been clear the moment he voiced his devotion to a specific type of person, a specific race. But she needed to hear him say it aloud.

"I'm so sorry. I never introduced myself. Please forgive me. I'm Nathaniel. Nathaniel Lark."

❖

The deputy director had a corner office with windows on both sides, allowing for a beautiful view of the Potomac River. Tyler looked over at Caden, who was checking her phone. She looked tired, mentally and physically. Tyler was going to say something, wanting to know what had taken place between her and Rowen, but her thoughts were interrupted by an opening door.

"Good morning, Agents." Martin came through the door carrying a white mug. It had the Department of Homeland Security Logo on the front with Deputy Director Martin written underneath. He pulled out his chair and took a seat behind the massive mahogany desk.

"Good morning, sir," they said in unison.

"What's the update?"

Caden answered. "There isn't a whole lot to update you on since yesterday, sir. Knight made contact last night and will be meeting with her contact today."

"When's she checking in?"

Caden shook her head. "She said she would text me. She thought it was too risky to wear a wire, and she didn't want to be under any time restraints. She thought it was the best approach."

He looked at Caden for a long moment. Tyler couldn't tell what he was thinking or if he approved of the plan. "What do you think, Styles?"

Caden shifted in her seat. "I think Knight knows these people better than us. I think we share a common goal, and I think we need to give her a bit of leeway. Let her shake the tree and see what falls out."

He looked at Tyler now. "Monroe?"

Tyler didn't like handing over control to another person. It made her uneasy. But she also trusted Caden, and Caden seemed to trust Rowen. "I agree with Agent Styles, sir. We need to see what Knight can come up with. Plus, it's a perfect time to see if the rootkit worked. Being able to verify that we have access to their computer system is crucial."

He stared at them both, taking a sip of his coffee. "Okay, I'm going to follow your lead on this one. Please keep me up to date. We can't afford to let this opportunity get by us. We need to get this guy before he manages to do any more damage."

Like we don't know that. Tyler just hoped that her initial thoughts about Rowen were incorrect and she really could help them the way she claimed she could.

Tyler and Caden headed to the car. They needed to be over at CIA headquarters to continue to work out the details. Hopefully, new messages had come in, and Jennifer and Brooke were able to sift through the information.

"How was your night?" Tyler asked.

"It was interesting." Caden's voice was monotone, very unlike her.

"Interesting?"

"I don't know what I was expecting. She's hard to read, hard to get a good handle on. But beyond that, I really do think she knows what she's doing when it comes to these guys. She had good reasons to not want the wire, and I believe they were genuine. I can't say why exactly, but I trust her, for the most part. I think she's holding shit back, but nothing that would affect the mission's outcome. Just typical agent walls, you know?"

Tyler nodded. Rowen was a mystery, and Tyler knew she intentionally played it that way. She kept everyone at a distance, and it was more than just job obligation. "You didn't sleep with her, did you?"

Caden briefly stopped walking and then caught up to Tyler a moment later. She smacked her in the arm. "No. I didn't sleep with her. Jesus, I'm not an animal."

Tyler looked at her sideways. "I didn't say you were. I just saw how you were looking at her, and, well, I know you."

Caden shoved her hands in her pockets, a tactic that Tyler had learned meant that she was a bit embarrassed. "Whatever. No, I didn't sleep with her."

Tyler hadn't meant to offend her, but that's apparently what she'd done. "I'm sorry. I didn't mean to upset you."

Caden's posture relaxed, but just slightly. "I don't hop into bed with *every* girl I meet."

Tyler put her hands up in a sign of surrender. "Okay, forget I said anything."

"I'm capable of having a meaningful relationship."

Tyler didn't understand where Caden's defensiveness was coming from. Typically, Caden would've laughed off the comment, but Tyler had clearly hit a nerve. "I know you are. I think it would be good for you. It's just not something I've seen from you yet."

"Maybe I want more."

Tyler was utterly confused. "From Rowen?"

Caden crossed her arms. Her posture said she was frustrated, and her expression was pained and contemplative. "No, not from

Rowen." She paused. "Just…just forget I said anything." Caden stormed away.

Tyler didn't know what mine field she had just stumbled into or what relationship nerve she had just hit. Caden was clearly struggling with something that she wasn't ready to talk about. Tyler wanted to offer some sort of reassurance, but she wasn't sure what to say. This was Brooke's area. Tyler was just learning to navigate the field of close relationships, and this behavior wasn't typical for Caden. She knew her response should entail support, and she should reiterate the fact that she was there if Caden needed to talk. "Okay, I'm here if you want to talk," she called. It didn't illicit a response, but she felt good about her attempt all the same. *That wasn't so hard.*

❖

Brooke started checking the log as soon as she had come in. If the rootkit worked, they would be closing in on Lark, finally. Jennifer had set the system to pull messages that used key terms, in hopes that it would help them sift through the flow of information that seemed to pour out of the system.

She looked up at the clock. Jennifer should have been there by now. It wasn't like her to be late for anything, much less today, when they would possibly be making progress. The door opened, and Rezentes came strolling through. She exhaled slowly, pulling herself together. She wouldn't show any weakness before this bastard; she didn't want him to know the effect he had on her. Then she took the time to really look at him. He was in the same clothes he had been in the day before. He clearly hadn't shaved, and he smelled more than usual, but the stench wasn't from his obnoxious cologne, it was from body odor, and that was definitely weird.

"I have Glass reassigned for the day, maybe longer."

Brooke stopped what she was doing and turned around in her chair. "You reassigned Glass?"

"That's what I said." His gaze was shifting around the room. He seemed uncomfortable, and that was out of character as well. He usually carried himself as if he owned the building.

Brooke knew something was off, so she kept talking to see if she could get to the bottom of it. "I just don't understand why. There are only a few of us assigned to this case, which makes it difficult enough. Glass is our best analyst. We need her."

"Tell you what, Hart, when you run your own task force, you can decide who goes where and for what reason. Until then, just do as you're told."

She turned back around in her chair. The conversation was clearly over, but it still didn't make any sense. Rezentes was an asshole, but putting himself first was what he did best, and having Glass on this case would benefit the outcome. The whole situation didn't add up, and she wanted to get a hold of Tyler to see what she thought.

As if she wished her into existence, Tyler came into the room, Caden right behind her. She gave her a smile before she spoke. "Anything yet?"

Brooke cleared her throat. "I'm going through it all now."

She heard Caden from behind her. "Where's Glass?"

Rezentes sighed obnoxiously. "The better question is, where is Knight? Everyone stop worrying about Glass. She's on special assignment."

"What's more important than this?" Caden had posed it as a question, but it was a statement, all the same.

"Don't worry about it. Where's Knight?"

Brooke wanted to turn around in her seat and watch the interaction, but she didn't dare. Rezentes was in a particularly bad mood this morning, and she didn't want to be on the receiving end of it.

When it was pretty obvious that Caden wasn't going to answer, Tyler did instead. "She'll check in with us when it's safe."

"I can't believe you two were put in charge of strategy. You send a foreign operative out on assignment with no plan, no check-in time. You know nothing. What a fucking waste."

The smirk on Tyler's face reflected her contempt for Rezentes. "We already briefed the director this morning about our intentions and the plan. If he wants you filled in, he'll direct us to do so or tell you on his own."

There was nothing he could say to that, not without looking like a fool. His face turned red, and he turned his attention away.

Brooke was doing a detailed search of the saved entries when the system dinged. A red label alert came through, meaning one of the top ten words Jennifer had programmed had just been used: "Knight." Brooke clicked on it and pulled it up onto the large monitor.

Brooke read the message out loud for everyone in the room. "Passed level four on the Dark Knight."

Rezentes pointed to the screen. "That could mean anything. It could be kids just talking about a stupid video game. Are you sure you two hooked this up right?"

"It makes sense they'd be talking in code. And even if it doesn't to you, it's worth investigating further. You don't want to be that guy," Caden said.

"What *guy* would that be?" he barked at her.

Caden answered without looking at him. "The guy that doesn't investigate every possible scenario, costing us a lead."

Caden had such a way with words, Brooke thought, almost laughing to herself.

"I'm going to call Glass and get her opinion on this." Caden went over to the other side of the room, phone to her ear. Rezentes followed closely behind Caden, creating the sense that he was her shadow, which Brooke knew would piss Caden off to no end.

Caden was back over a few moments later, Rezentes still far too close to her. She threw him an irritated glance before saying to the others, "She didn't answer. Maybe you should try her, Brooke. She might be ignoring me."

Rezentes waved his arms in front of him. "No, no one contacts Glass. Just focus on your own jobs. Learn to follow orders." He stormed out of the room, leaving the three of them staring at each other.

"What's his problem?" Tyler asked.

"You mean besides the obvious? That he's clearly compensating, smells like the ass end of a dump, and has the intelligence of swamp moss?" Caden asked, leaning against the wall.

Brooke rocked back and forth in her chair. "I can't believe there's anything more important than this mission right now. What else would he possibly assign Jen to?"

Tyler rubbed the back of her neck. "Doesn't make any sense."

Caden pointed at the screen. "Brooke, can't you track her or something?"

"It doesn't work like that. We don't arbitrarily place tracking devices on analysts."

Caden was pacing, agitated, plus she seemed worried. "Something is up."

Caden was right. Something was off. Even if Jennifer had been reassigned, she would have called her, at the very least to complain about Rezentes. She thought about taking Caden's advice and calling, but she didn't want to deal with her boss's wrath. But then again, this wouldn't have been the first time Jennifer had kept a mission to herself. It could be that everything was on the up-and-up. There was no way to know for sure, so the only thing Brooke could do at this point was to focus on what was in front of her. She looked at the messages scrolling over the screen and did her best to push the worry she felt to the back of her mind. It might be a temporary solution, but right now, it was all she had.

CHAPTER SIXTEEN

Jennifer sat in a lavish, distastefully decorated office. The walls were littered with bright, extravagant pieces of artwork. The images reminded her of fire, anger, and death. She thought of how appropriate that was. She had only taken a few psychology classes is college, but she knew that she was being left alone in this room for two reasons. The first was to make her anxious; the second was to assert his authority. He wanted to make it clear he was the one in charge.

"Ms. Glass, thank you for coming by." He took a seat at his ostentatious desk.

"You make it sound like I had a choice."

"Oh now, Ms. Glass, we always have a choice. And you have made the right one."

"I haven't agreed to anything."

"Not yet, but if the answer was going to be no, you wouldn't be sitting here right now. You would have walked out of the facility and run to your little friends."

"And my sister would be dead. That's not much of a choice."

"Yes. See! You get it now! I knew you were smart!" He pounded his desk with his hands, emphasizing his enthusiasm. His voice was filled with laughter, joy, a kid on Christmas morning. It was disgusting.

"Why me?"

"Why you? Why you?" His voice got louder with each question. "Because we think you are the key, Ms. Glass. You're the key we've been missing. You're going to help us make all our dreams come true."

Jennifer noted the plural phrasing. She also wondered if he was aimlessly referring to some obscure voices in his head. "I don't know what I can possibly do for you."

His grin widened. His teeth were white, cosmetically so. It was a stark contrast to his absurdly tanned, slightly orange skin. Everything about this man was fake. "Don't you worry, Ms. Glass. I'm going to let you know exactly when the cause needs you."

"And what makes you think I won't leave here and turn you in?"

He walked his fingers across the desk until his arm was fully extended, then he pointed at her and smiled. "Because if you do, I won't just kill your sister, I will dismember her. I'll pull her apart bit by bit, and you will hear her screams every time you close your eyes."

Pricks of pain washed over her body, like tiny needles pressing into every pore on her skin. "If you so much as touch her, I'll—"

He laughed, a full and powerful joyful laugh that came from the depths of his belly. "You'll do what? Kill me? Let's ignore the fact that you don't have it in you." He waved his hand in dismissal. "Don't forget who brought you here. Your boss is on our payroll. He believes in the cause. And of course he believes in the money that will come his way once we've done what we need to do. Do you really believe it stops at him, though? Styles, Monroe, Hart, they all report to someone, and I've got ears everywhere. It will get back to me before any of you has a chance to do anything, and that will piss me off." He unwrapped a butterscotch candy from a dish that sat on his desk and popped it in his mouth. "Do you really want to bet your sister's life on who can get there first?" He smiled at her, the candy placed firmly between his teeth. "So, like I said, I'll let you know when I need you."

"So that's it? Are you going to let me go? Head back to the CIA? I'm supposed to just sit around and what? Wait for you to blow up the world?"

"Blow up the world? That's insane. I don't want to blow up the world."

"Then what *do* you want?"

He ticked his finger back and forth. "Tsk, tsk, tsk. All in good time."

He pushed a button on his phone, and four very large men entered the room. "I'm very sorry about this, but please understand, precautions must be taken."

She didn't get the chance to fully turn around before a black bag was placed over her head. She was hauled up out of her seat, her hands thrust behind her back, and placed in restraints. They dragged her through the building, her feet barely touching the floor.

Fear and anger surged through her as she attempted to fight back. She knew it was a futile attempt, but she had to do something. She didn't want to be helpless or a pawn in someone else's game. But in this moment, that's exactly what she was, and she hated him even more for it.

Caden checked her phone again. She didn't know who she wanted to hear from more, Rowen or Jennifer. There was no reason to think Jennifer would contact her, but she hoped all the same. It didn't make sense that she wasn't there today, and it made even less sense that Rezentes would have reassigned her to anything. He needed her to make himself look good.

The vibration in her hand sent a jolt of relieved anticipation up her body. It was Rowen, and she wanted her to come over. Well, probably not *wanted*, but it was part of the plan. She grabbed her jacket off the back of a chair and glanced out the window. Jennifer was staggering past, her gaze on the ground in front of her, her arms wrapped tightly around herself. It was the same way she had seen her after the night they had spent together. *She's scared.*

She hurried downstairs and called her name. Jennifer stopped but didn't turn around, though her posture stiffened. Caden ran up alongside her.

"Hey!"

Jennifer's face was tight, and she wouldn't make eye contact. "What's up?"

Caden touched her shoulder. "Where were you today?"

"I had some personal stuff to do." She started down the sidewalk.

Caden took a few steps to catch up with her. "Some personal stuff? Rezentes said you were assigned somewhere else for the day."

Jennifer wouldn't look her in the eye. She wouldn't even turn her face toward her. "I don't want to talk about it."

Something was very wrong, and Caden felt a pang of protectiveness rush through her. "Jen, hey, what's going on? You can talk to me."

She looked at her now, her eyes filled with tears. She wiped them away with more force than what was necessary. "Leave me alone, Caden. I don't feel like talking." She started to walk again.

"Then we won't talk. Let's just go upstairs. We can watch a movie or something."

She huffed. There was annoyance and anger in her sigh. "It's not going to happen. I'm not going to sleep with you."

Caden crossed her arms. "Okay. Understood. But let's just go inside."

Jennifer looked up and down the street like she was searching for something, then back at Caden. "Okay. Fine." She turned around and started stalking back toward Caden's apartment.

"Great, Caden. Sounds like fun, Caden. Thanks for inviting me, Caden. That's so nice of you, Caden." She wanted to make Jennifer smile, but her words had no effect.

Once they reached the apartment, Caden headed straight for the bathroom. She pulled out her phone and texted Rowen, letting her know that she would be a little late. She knew Rowen wouldn't argue with her; she was too aloof for that.

When she came out, Jennifer was staring out the window adjacent to the kitchen. Caden wanted to be near her but didn't want to overwhelm her, so she busied herself by opening the cabinet and looked at the tea she had bought the day after the night she had spent with Jennifer. A purchase made in a moment of blind hope that she would come back and spend the night again.

After a few moments, Jennifer went over to the breakfast bar that separated the kitchen from the living room. Caden felt her eyes on her.

"What are you doing?"

"Making you tea." She said it without turning around.

"Do you have anything stronger?"

Caden didn't know what was going on, but it wasn't good. "You know I do. Is beer okay?" She didn't want to start drinking anything harder. There was a lot going on, and they both needed to be sharp.

"Beer is fine." Jennifer curled up on the couch.

Caden popped the top off two bottles and handed Jennifer one. She sat on the opposite end of the leather couch, intentionally keeping her distance.

"Are you going to tell me what's going on?"

Jennifer took a long sip of her beer. "No."

Caden didn't know how to maneuver through this line of questioning. Normally, someone would leave a little space for dancing around a subject, an opening for questions. The quick and resolute "no," allowed for no such calculated steering.

"How's your mom doing?" Jennifer asked.

Caden watched as Jennifer took another sip of beer. She didn't understand why Jennifer wanted to talk about her mom when something was clearly going on, but she was going to let her change the subject anyway. "She's doing good. Feeling much better. The biopsy came back negative."

"I'm so glad to hear that. I was thinking about her just last week."

Caden had only ever mentioned the issues with her mom to Jennifer the one night they had spent together. She couldn't believe that she had not only remembered, but had been actively thinking about it. The knowledge warmed her chest. "Yeah, she's talking about coming up here in a few months."

"Ugh, tell her not to come here in the summer. The humidity is brutal."

Caden laughed. "Jen, she spent the first fourteen years of her life in Puerto Rico and most of her adult life in Florida. She'll be fine."

"I can picture you as a kid, running around at the beach. Bringing home more sand in your swimsuit than any parent wants to deal with. I bet you were into everything."

"I was a handful."

"You're still a handful."

"Thank you." She winked, which would have typically elicited an eye roll, but nothing came.

Jennifer's expression was nothing but worry. She sat a bit slumped over, looking defeated. Still, she was beautiful. Caden had told her as much once and was met with disbelief. The list of negative attributes she had ticked off in response was enough to fill a truck. She wondered who had convinced her she wasn't the beautiful person she was, just as she was wondering now, who had put her in such distress.

"Where did your parents meet? I mean, I remember you telling me that your mom's family had lived in Florida, but your dad?"

"My dad was born in Ohio. They met when he was stationed in Florida with the Coast Guard. My mom was eighteen, and he was twenty. They will be married thirty-five years this October. Still run around together like teenagers."

"Ohio? How did he end up in the Coast Guard?"

"Probably because he's from Ohio. A lot of people join the military because they want something different. The Coast Guard is a far stretch from Ohio."

"How long was he in for?"

"Twenty-five years. Why the sudden interest in my family?"

Jennifer looked contemplative. "I was just thinking about mine today. Thinking about how much I miss them."

Caden waited for her to go on, hoping that Jennifer might be steeling herself to talk, to tell her what was really going on with her.

"My parents, unlike yours, never got along. My dad was a mean drunk. He had a cruel mouth and a heavy hand. My mom tried to get him help. I think he was in seven or eight rehabs by the time I was eight. It wasn't until he got drunk one night and tossed both me and my little sister down the stairs, that she left. Then we kind of bounced around from place to place, always trying to hide from him. My mom never made a lot of money, but she did the best she could. We never stayed anywhere long enough for her to earn any promotions. She's smart though, tough, and determined."

"Sounds a lot like you."

The only indication that Jennifer had heard her was the barest flicker of a smile that crossed her lips. Her eyes focused on some unidentifiable spot across the room.

"I was mad at her. Can you believe that? Mad that we kept moving, mad that I couldn't stay with the friends I had made, mad that I would fall behind in school, mad about the things we couldn't afford. There she was, doing her very best to take care of us, to provide for us, and I was such a brat."

"You were a kid."

"That doesn't feel like an adequate excuse."

"Well, you were a kid. You don't feel like that now. She knows how much you love her. You and your sister have turned out to be successful and smart women. I mean, you went to NYU and your sister is at Georgetown. She did something right."

Jennifer's eyes filled with tears. "My sister's going to be a civil rights attorney. Can you believe that?"

"I can." She scooted over on the couch and placed a hand on her back. She rubbed in what she hoped was a soothing motion, though she hadn't had a lot of experience trying to make someone feel better. "I know your mom lives in Virginia, but you never mentioned your dad. Where is he now?"

She sniffled, wiping tears from her eyes. "He's been dead for years. Cirrhosis of the liver."

Caden didn't say she was sorry because she wasn't, and she knew instinctively that Jennifer didn't miss him. "Why don't you just call your sister and get together for lunch? Things have been busy lately, but you can certainly make time for lunch. I know how close you two are. I'm sure if you had something planned to go see her, you would feel better. Maybe not miss her so much."

Jennifer's eyes were fixed on her own now. Caden focused on keeping her breathing under control. Their faces were so close, she could feel Jennifer's breath on her lips.

"I can't." She stood up fast, pushing past Caden. "I have to go."

Caden stood and tried to cut her off at the door. "Jen, please don't go. Tell me what's going on."

She stopped at the door, her back still facing her. "Why, Caden?" She turned around and looked like she desperately wanted a real answer. "Why should I stay here with you?"

Caden didn't know whether to tell the truth or not. She hadn't expected her plea to work, but now she was forced to confront a whirlwind of emotions she hadn't been expecting to deal with.

The feelings she had always had for Jennifer were still there. They were so close to the surface, slicking her skin as if it were a barrier of sweat. It was possibly the last remaining barrier of resistance against the woman a foot away. Jennifer's face was so desperate, so pained. She wanted to tell her that everything would be okay, that she was here for her. She wanted to be the one to put a smile on her face, not just tonight but a week, a month, a year from now. But nothing came out. All she could do was stare, overwhelmed by the sudden desire to be the one someone would turn to in moments like these.

"Have a good night, Caden."

Just like that, she was gone. Caden's chest burned. She put her head against the door. *Why are you such a damn coward?* This would have been the perfect opportunity to prove not only to Jennifer, but to herself as well that she was capable of more than just a one-night stand. She could have opened herself up to her; she could have been vulnerable. Jennifer could be trusted with that, and she wanted to show her she trusted her with that type of exposure. But again, she'd missed her chance. *How many more of those do I expect to get?*

CHAPTER SEVENTEEN

Brooke wasn't sure what to expect from the encounter. The diner was busy, as it always was on a Saturday morning. People were laughing, talking, and minding their own business. There were clanging dishes, yells from the kitchen, and the sound of Brooke's own heart thumping in her chest. When she told her dad that she would be patient with her mom, she didn't expect to be meeting them a day later. She sipped her coffee and ran her hand up and down Tyler's leg.

Tyler grabbed her hand as her mother came through the door, her dad not far behind. She looked overdressed for this small diner. Her blue skirt and matching jacket seemed to illuminate her arrogance. She slid into the booth and sat across from them, placing her purse by her side. Her impeccable outfit would have led anyone to believe that her mom had it all together, but her eyes were shadowed with worry, a look Brooke wasn't accustomed to seeing on her. She almost asked if she was okay but decided better of it. Her father gave her a small smile and nodded at Tyler.

"Thank you for meeting us." Her mother's tone was professional and collected. She may as well have been marking the beginning of a business meeting. "The reason we came here was because we wanted to discuss something with you, and regardless of what has transpired, we need to finish that conversation."

Brooke waited for them to continue. Tyler gripped her hand a little tighter under the table, knowing that she needed some additional support.

Her father cleared his throat. His face was tired, and he looked older than he ever had. "We came here because I had a job interview. I've been offered a position working for the Secretary of the Navy, overseeing an intelligence division. I wanted you to know that I'm going to take it."

"You're going to be living here?" Brooke wasn't sure how she felt about the revelation.

"Congratulations, sir," Tyler said a little too enthusiastically.

"Thank you, Gunnery Sergeant." He paused for a moment. "Sorry, Special Agent."

Brooke stared at her mother. Her face held no real expression. "What do you think, Mom?"

She waved at the server, who immediately brought over her coffee. Her mother always had a way of commanding a room and getting exactly what she wanted. "Oh, you know me. I want whatever your father wants."

"That's not really an answer."

She tore open a small cream container and poured it into her coffee. "It is an answer, Brooke. I have spent a lifetime supporting your father, and that doesn't suddenly stop."

"But how do you feel about it?"

She sighed, seemingly annoyed by Brooke's question. "I feel fine about it, Brooke. We are having our belongings packed up as we speak. We should have everything here within the month."

"When do you start, sir?" Tyler asked.

"I start on Monday. This interview was just a formality."

"Congratulations, Dad. This will help you get your foot in the political door. That's what you have always wanted. That will give the four of us the chance to spend more time together." She could try to be positive about this situation. That's what Tyler would do, and maybe it would help improve their relationship.

Her mother spoke before her dad had a chance. "Just because we let you know our plans, doesn't change anything. You need to grow up, Brooke. It's probably my fault. I wasn't hard enough on you. Everything has always come so easy for you. You seem to think that everything will always fall into place. But that's not the way the world works. I'm sure Tyler is a very nice girl, but this won't work." She pointed to them both. "You'll grow bored of her the way you did with your toys as a child and move on to the next. Eventually, you'll grow up and realize the only acceptable thing to do is to settle down with a man, just as God intended."

"Janice, I don't think—"

Her mom didn't let him finish his thought. "We didn't raise you to be this."

"And what is this?" Brooke's heart was racing. Her hands started to shake, and she could feel her chest begin to heave.

She snorted. "You're a smart girl, Brooke. I don't need to spell it out for you. But just to be clear, I will. We didn't raise you to be an abomination. You two are a punch line to a very tired joke, and I don't want it in my family. I won't have it."

"Since when did you become such a religious zealot?" Brooke seethed. "We didn't go to church. You made fun of the people who did. What's this really about?"

Her mom tossed her napkin on the table and sat back in her chair. "Don't be a petulant brat, Brooke. I don't need to attend church every week to believe and embrace the teachings of the Bible."

Brooke was about to unleash a string of thoughts she hadn't quite yet formed. She felt Tyler's hand squeeze around hers.

"Mrs. Hart, your daughter is many things. She is kind, compassionate, incredibly smart, accepting, and supportive. She's shown me that I'm capable of things I never dreamed possible. I'm a better person for having her in my life, and I'm positive our friends would say the same thing. I know you're upset and I know you need some time to come to terms with this reality. I also know you believe what you're doing and saying is the right thing. I know this because I see the same passion and determination in your eyes that I see in Brooke's when she makes her mind up about something. I know I'm not good enough for your daughter. I also know I'm going to spend the rest of my life trying to prove the contrary. Not to please you or Captain Hart, but because that's what Brooke deserves. You have raised someone who knows her worth, knows what she wants, and won't settle for anything less. So this might not be the life that you envisioned for her, I might not be the person you had hoped for, but she is who she is and I'm who she has chosen. And because you have raised someone who will be who she is in the face of adversity, regardless of who stands in front of her. It's not something you can wish away. Brooke is gay, and she'd continue to be gay even if I weren't in the picture. That's reality, and to lose someone as incredible as your daughter over your inability to cope with who she loves, would be a true travesty."

Tyler's phone buzzed for the fourth time, and she looked down at it. She nudged Brooke, and they both slid out of the booth. Tyler extended her hand to Brooke's father and he took it. "Congratulations again, sir." She smiled at Brooke's mom. "I hope to see you again under better circumstances, Mrs. Hart. Good luck with the move."

They left the diner, and Brooke could only think of one thing to say, so she said it. "I love you."

CHAPTER EIGHTEEN

Jennifer watched the messages move across the screen without actually seeing them. All she could think about was her sister. She wanted to contact her, to warn her, but she didn't know what would happen if she did. She assumed they were watching her every move. Any indiscretion could end with her sister being killed. She couldn't go to anyone in the agency. Lark had made it perfectly clear that his reach was vast, that he had people in his corner, people with more power and more pull than she would ever wield. Of course, she could talk to Caden, Tyler, and Brooke. She was sure they could keep it between themselves and figure out a way to move forward. She'd been close to discussing it with Caden the night before. The issue that stopped her then and what was stopping her now, was that she knew they would help. If they made this even more personal than it already was, they could get themselves hurt too, and that would be on her. The weight of the realization was crushing; in order to protect the people she cared about, she needed to keep this to herself and figure out what to do next. *Am I really capable of helping this man?*

She tried to focus on what she knew, and that list was short. The piece she was struggling to put into place was why Carol O'Brien, the Speaker of the House, was concerned about Rowen, and how they were all tied to Lark.

The door beeped and Jennifer held her breath. She let it out when Brooke and Tyler came through the door.

"Whoa, what's wrong? You look like you just saw a ghost."

"I thought you were Rezentes."

Brooke shook her head. "Is he going to try to reassign you again? What happened to you, anyway?"

Jennifer stared at Brooke and Tyler. She wanted to tell them everything that had happened. She wanted their input, but she said nothing. Fear gripped the back of her throat, making it impossible to speak. No, she wouldn't tell them. She needed to figure this out on her own. She wouldn't jeopardize them. "Just some bullshit assignment. I'm back now."

Brooke gave her a look that indicated she didn't fully believe her, but she took a seat next to her anyway. She started looking over the messages on the screen. "Anything of any importance hit?"

Jennifer's chest burned. She pushed it to the back of her mind and turned in her seat, facing the computer screen. "No, not yet." Lark expected her to just go about her business until he told her what he wanted. She felt like a traitor, not just to her organization, but to her friends as well. *That's because you are, idiot.*

She heard Tyler's voice from behind them. "I hate waiting. We need to do something."

A few moments later, Caden walked into the room. She looked like something was wrong, and Jennifer felt guilty. Last night, Caden had tried to be her friend. She wanted to be there for her, and Jennifer had shut her down. Not because she had wanted to, but because she didn't know what else to do.

Tyler pulled up a chair closer to Jennifer and Brooke. "Okay, I know we've done this a thousand times before, but not since we had Rowen. Let's look at everything we know."

Caden sat next to Tyler and rubbed her eyes. "The one thing that has never made sense to me is where Lark gets his money from. Yes, the National Socialist Movement has plenty of funding, but not the kind to support this type of operation. We know he has embezzled money through dummy corporations, funded by phony and real stocks. The problem with bringing him in on any of those charges is that he's a ghost. He has people go to meetings for him, make deals for him, and we can't find anyone willing to identify him. Even when we had Thompson in custody last year, he chose death over identification."

Tyler interrupted. "The money we've been able to trace still isn't enough to fund an organization like this. He has the ability to erect underground camps and mobile homes throughout the country, according to Rowen. It's possible that a large portion of his funding is coming from overseas organizations with the same ideology. And if that's the case, we really have no idea how far this goes or how deep their reach is. We started following social media accounts where he spilled his rhetoric, along with sites on the dark Web, but he's always one step ahead."

Brooke stared at the picture of Thompson on the screen. She was tapping a pen against her cheek and her focus was intense. "What does everything point to? This isn't a normal terror organization. Yes, he wants it to seem that way on the surface, but it's not. He has always focused on the upper levels of government. He was after CIA assets and evacuation procedures for the executive branch when he hit the Farm. What does that tell us? He could cause more mayhem and unrest by going after citizens and landmarks, so why is he focused on these things?"

Tyler added to Brooke's thoughts. "This isn't a National Socialist Movement play. They want to cause civil unrest, start a race war. They want angry white people in the streets, guns in tow. That's not big government stuff."

Jennifer turned in her chair, adrenaline flushing through her body. The pieces were starting to fall together. Maybe there was a way out of this without endangering her sister. She started typing and talking at the same time. "We've been assuming that Lark is in charge of everything. What if he's not? What if he's the front man for someone else? What if Rowen is right, and it goes a lot higher than him, within our own government?"

Tyler stood and began to pace. "That would make sense. Rowen explained how the organization was built up. With that much secrecy, it would make sense that Lark wasn't the name at the top. Why go through all of that to let your name out there?"

Jennifer continued her thought. "Lark has nothing to really gain by all of this chaos."

Caden didn't seem convinced. "True, but information is priceless. If he succeeded in being able to uncover the secrets of the United States government, there are a dozen countries that would pay for that information. Probably more."

Jennifer couldn't tell them everything she knew, but she could divulge a small piece of information. "I saw Speaker O'Brien in the parking garage the other day. She was talking to someone, but I couldn't see who."

"What do you mean you couldn't see who? If you saw her there talking, you must have seen a face." Caden looked incredulous.

Jennifer hoped she didn't look as guilty as she felt. "I didn't think to check at the time." She knew it was a ridiculous answer, but she didn't have time to come up with anything else. She just hoped they would let it slide, so she could push this in the right direction.

"What are you saying?" Brooke asked.

"Okay, what if we look at it by filling in our own blanks, just for now. Let's look at things from a different angle and see if it holds any weight. We knew what was in those files he was after—CIA personnel, assets, and plausible evacuation proce-dures for the executive branch. What if he was specifically after the evacuation information, and the CIA records were just there to throw us off, make us think he wanted whatever information he could get his hands on? If you knew the evacuation proce-dures for the executive branch, if you knew exactly where they would take the president and vice president in the event of an attack or how they would protect them, you could, in theory, foil the procedure. If someone really wanted to, they could ensure their demise with that information. With that kind of knowledge, you could create a power vacuum."

"Who, specifically, would benefit from the deaths of the president and vice president?" Brooke asked.

"Think about the line of succession. If the president and vice president are killed, or even taken hostage, who takes over?"

Tyler's face turned white. "The Speaker of the House."

Brooke wiped her hands across her face. "Holy shit. Carol O'Brien."

Caden got closer to the circle. "We can't detain the Speaker of the House, and that's an awful lot of assumption just because you saw her talking to someone in our parking lot."

Jennifer put her hand up, keeping her voice just above a whisper. "Is it though? Think about it. The Speaker has made three failed attempts at the presidency, but has never been able to nab the nomination."

"Because she's a maniac. No one wants to see her in charge, even the staunch Republicans. The only reason she's even the Speaker is because of her fundraising abilities that derive from the alt-right and quite possibly her overseas party connections. She has one of the largest charities on the planet, and you don't really think all that money goes to the pro-life movement. She holds all the Republicans in the house hostage with threats of pulling monetary support. The only way she will ever be president is if she, quite literally, takes it by force."

Caden didn't seem convinced. "Charitable donations are still regulated. She can't just filter money to wherever she wants, not the kind of money it would take to execute an organization of this magnitude."

"Not really. Money from her organization is often filtered to other charities. If the amounts aren't in large enough sums, they wouldn't raise any red flags. It's not that difficult to set up a nonprofit. What if Lark helped her set up dummy nonprofits, the same way he set up dummy corporations? And if there's foreign money involved, who knows how hard it would be to trace?" Brooke said.

Caden leaned across the table. "That's a huge accusation to lob at the Speaker with no real proof. The end result could be catastrophic for all our careers."

Jennifer knew Caden was right. They would need more evidence. They needed *her* evidence. She desperately wanted to tell them. She needed to tell them, but could she really risk her sister? "Look, we were told to run down every possible lead. I have a gut feeling about this, and I need you to trust me. I'll try to put more pieces together here, but I need your help running leads in the field."

Caden stared at her for a long moment. She could tell by the way her body was slightly shifting that her leg was rocking up and down under the table. She was considering what Jennifer had said to her. "Shit. We need to report to Deputy Director Martin, and you two need to tell Rezentes." She pointed between Brooke and Jennifer.

Jennifer's stomach dropped. "Why don't we hold off on telling Rezentes? Just until we really know if we're on the right track. You know how he is. This could blow up."

Caden nodded at Tyler. "What do you think?"

Tyler stared at Brooke for a long moment before she spoke. "I think we have to talk to the deputy director, but it's up to them if they want to fill Rezentes in. We don't report to him."

Brooke shrugged. "It's Saturday and he's made it pretty clear he doesn't like to be bothered on weekends. We don't *have* to say anything until Monday."

Jennifer was weak with relief. "Besides, it will give us some time to figure out if we're on the right track."

Tyler leaned down, kissing the top of Brooke's head. Brooke closed her eyes, and Jennifer knew that she was taking in the strength Tyler emitted. She glanced at Caden, offering a half smile. Caden shoved her hands into her pockets and turned away.

It pained Jennifer to watch Caden go without being able to explain, but there wasn't an alternative. If she wasn't going to tell them what was happening, she couldn't risk being alone with Caden. *Stop being an angst-filled teenager and get to work. You can deal with all of this other crap later.* She just hoped that once it was all over, her friends would understand why she'd made the decision she had. *Will they accept that I couldn't trust them with this?*

Chapter Nineteen

Tyler waited patiently in the coffee shop where she and Caden had asked Rowen to meet them. It was conveniently located right across the street from headquarters, so even if Rowen was being followed, it would make sense to be there, seeing as she was playing the angle of double agent and supposedly sleeping with Caden.

Rowen entered the coffee shop, and Tyler watched her search the surrounding faces, finally falling on her own. She noted the look of disappointment when Rowen recognized her. *Hoping it was Caden, perhaps?*

"She went to the bathroom," Tyler said to Rowen as she sat down, still looking around.

Rowen looked mad at the implication that she had been looking for Caden. "What's up? We shouldn't be seen together."

Tyler smiled. "If you're supposedly sleeping with my best friend, wouldn't it make sense that you would be having coffee with her and her best friend?"

Rowen didn't say anything. The question was rhetorical. "Did you guys figure anything out?"

Tyler couldn't help but smile as she thought back on the progress they had recently made. "We may have a lead."

Caden came from behind one of the corners and took a seat at the table. Tyler paid particular attention to the way Rowen watched her move. Her eyes traveled up and down, tracking each movement Caden made.

Caden took her seat, her eyes fixed on Rowen. "Hi."

Rowen watched Caden's lips. "Hi."

Tyler filed the information away to ponder over later. "Okay, here's what we know—" Tyler stopped when Rowen's jaw clenched, and her eyes narrowed slightly as she looked over Tyler's shoulder. Still, she wasn't prepared for the two men that were upon them in moments, interrupting the conversation. They pulled Caden out of her chair and turned her around. Tyler stood up to protest, and they pushed her back down into her seat. "Caden Styles, you're under arrest for treason."

They clamped handcuffs around her wrists. "What are you talking about? I'm a special agent with Homeland Security." She tried to pull her arms free. "Let me show you my badge."

"There's no need. We know who you are."

"You're making a serious mistake," Tyler said. She tried to stand again, and the man to her side gave her a warning look. "Where are you taking her?"

The men said nothing else as they dragged Caden out of the coffee shop. Caden turned to look at them, her expression both pissed off and confused.

Tyler pulled out her phone and dialed a number. She looked at Rowen. "Let's go."

They hurried down the busy streets, practically in a full out run back to headquarters.

When they made it back, Tyler pushed the elevator button over and over again. She knew there was no point to it, but the motion made her feel like she was accomplishing something. Which was better than doing nothing as her best friend was being hauled off to a jail cell for something she wasn't capable of participating in. Rowen, standing stiffly next to her, said nothing. She looked just as confused, and Tyler was slightly comforted by that.

They found Brooke and Jennifer where she had left them; the only difference now was that Rezentes also occupied the room. It didn't matter. Nothing mattered except finding out what was going on.

"Caden was just arrested."

"What?" they said in unison.

Tyler paced back and forth, needing the movement to help settle her mind. "They just walked in and put handcuffs on her. She's being charged with treason."

She heard Rezentes let out a small chuckle. "Figures."

Tyler knew even as she strode over to him that she shouldn't touch him. She knew intellectually it would accomplish nothing except to give him the upper hand. Her body, on the other hand, didn't seem to care about her internal reflection. She put her hand around his neck and pushed him backward, and kept pushing until his back hit the wall. His hands were batting at her arm in an unsuccessful attempt to get her to release him.

"What did you say?" The question came out as a breath. She said it into the side of his face, her body surging with anger and betrayal.

Brooke tugged at her shoulder. "You have to let him go."

Tyler didn't want to let him go. She wanted to continue to squeeze until he passed out. She wanted him to understand what it's like to be a loyal friend and what it means when you cross the line. His face was red, puffy, and he was struggling. Brooke pulled at her shoulder again. She released her grip and he crumpled onto the floor.

He was gasping for air and coughing. His hand moved to his neck and rubbed the spot where Tyler's hand had just been. "You're done, Monroe. I'm going to have your ass thrown in jail."

Jennifer stood next to Brooke. "No, that's not what you're going to do."

Rezentes spit on the ground, the coughing still breaking up his normal tone. "Fuck you, Glass. You're all done. You all stood around and watched this happen. You'll be lucky if you get a job at Best Buy after this."

Jennifer crossed her arms. "Then I'll tell everyone that you Tasered me, put me in the trunk of a car, and had me taken to your boss, Lark."

Rezentes tried to stand. Tyler grabbed him and threw him into a chair. "Sit there and don't move."

She looked at Jennifer. "You need to start from the beginning."

❖

When Jennifer had finally finished rehashing the entire story, she was exhausted. She had no idea what it meant for her sister, but with Caden in jail and Rezentes threatening Tyler, she had to make a decision. When she had made the decision not to tell anyone, part of the reason was because she was worried about putting them in danger, but now they were in danger anyway. *Caden* was in danger, and that was unacceptable. It was a calculated risk but one she had to take. Luckily, the only person who knew she had said anything was sitting in a chair against his will.

"You should have told me." Brooke's tone was hurt.

"I couldn't." Jennifer knew it wasn't an adequate answer, but she wasn't sure what else to say. "If they were able to get to my sister, they could get to all of you, and your families too. I couldn't put any of you in danger like that. Which seems stupid now, seeing that Caden is in jail for treason, of all things. They're going after you anyway. Hopefully, we can figure out how to keep my sister safe, now that you know." Jennifer looked at the group, hoping they'd not only forgive her silence, but help her as well. "This is how I know O'Brien is involved, but I couldn't tell you as much before. I couldn't get much out of Lark, but he's clearly involved with O'Brien. The only thing that makes sense in my head is that it has something to do with putting her in power. Otherwise, why would she risk involvement? And we know Lark wanted the executive evacuation plans. If you put them together, it makes sense."

"Here's what we're going to do." Tyler stood with purpose. "I'm going to go send two guys to pick up your sister. We're going to bring her here until this is all over, so we know she's safe. You two are going to start digging around in the dark Web. Someone is doing all of this IT work for Lark and O'Brien, right? It's not like they could do it on their own. If we can find those people and convince them that we have enough on them to prosecute, maybe we can get them to flip. If they can give us the information we need, that will lead to the final resting place of the messages being sent, we'll find Lark. Once we have Lark, we'll be able to find out just what he and O'Brien are plotting, then we can go after her. We can't hit that main outpost without knowing for certain he's in there. If we spook him, he'll be in the wind and we'll never get another chance like this. But we'll damn well find people who can bring him down after we've caught him. No one with any sense will want to be caught up in this when the dust settles, and we're about to kick up a lot of it."

Rowen rubbed the back of her neck, looking distracted and stressed. Jennifer had a sense that she knew more than she was letting on. The thought made Jennifer's skin prick with agitation.

"If you pick up her sister, they're going to know."

Tyler crossed her arms and stared at her. "Why do you say that?"

Rowen looked at Jennifer as she spoke. "Because they've been following her for a long time. There's someone following her now. I know because I was one of the people assigned to the task. That's where I've been the last few days. I didn't tell any of you because I figured I could manage the situation if I was part of it." She stared at a spot on the wall, clearly not wanting to make eye contact with anyone. "When they make threats against someone's family, they aren't bluffing. They have those people watched constantly, so they know exactly where they are if they need to make a move to keep someone in line. When I tell you their reach is extensive, I'm probably not giving them enough credit. They can get to anyone at any time."

"What the hell? Who else have you been watching?" Brooke yelled at her.

Rowen clasped her hands together and took a moment before she answered. "All of you. I have been watching each and every one of you. That was my assignment from Lark, and I've been doing it for about a month."

"What about our families?" Jennifer expected Tyler's voice to hold a bit more anger, but there wasn't any there, not that she could tell anyway. She couldn't understand how Tyler could be so calm.

"I know all about your families, but I haven't been watching them. With the exception of Jennifer's sister."

"What did you hope to gain?" Tyler asked.

"I wasn't trying to gain anything except Lark's trust, which I did."

"Why didn't you tell us sooner? You could have divulged this at any point, on any day you've been here."

Rowen looked up at Tyler, who was now standing over her. "Oh, I could have? Then what? You would have let me work on this with you? No, you would have thrown my ass out the door."

"I still might throw your ass out the door," Brooke said.

"Look, I told you, and I didn't have to do that. That should count for something. But listen to me when I say they're not bluffing."

Jennifer had questions that needed to be answered too. "Did you know they took me? That they were going to take Caden?"

Rowen put her hands up in defense. "No, of course not."

"Of course not? How are we supposed to believe you? You just admitted to watching my sister, to watching all of us, though you never mentioned it before, and now we're just supposed to take your word for it?"

"Look, I care about Caden too, and I don't want to see anything happen to her, which is why I'm even bothering to have this conversation. We need to get your sister out of danger and we need to get him before Caden's fate is out of all our hands. Yes, I lied to you, or more accurately, withheld the truth. But the only reason I did that was because it wasn't important. You might not see it that way, but it wasn't. If I had told you, you wouldn't have listened to me, and we wouldn't be working together. You should be glad it was me and not someone else. I never gave him anything that would jeopardize any of you. Sometimes we have to do things we don't want for the greater good of the mission."

Jennifer knew she wasn't capable of physically hurting Rowen, who was a highly trained agent, and the only skills Jennifer had were obtained from a six-week class she had taken with Tyler. None of that mattered here in this moment. She was going to hit Rowen Knight, and no one was going to be able to stop her. She moved across the room with determination and anger surging through her body. Her sole focus was on Rowen and Rowen knew it. She watched her come but didn't move into a defensive position.

Brooke stepped in front of her, putting her hands up. "I know you're pissed, but this isn't the time or place. We need to get your sister out of there, we need to help Caden, and we need to figure out what we are going to do about him." She nodded toward Rezentes in the corner. Tyler had placed zip ties around his wrists and a piece of duct tape over his mouth.

Jennifer stared at Rowen. Her breathing was erratic, and she could taste the adrenaline in the back of her throat, metallic and dry. "I knew we couldn't trust you. You should have told me."

Rowen put her hands up, indicating her surrender. "I was going to, but I couldn't just run over here as soon as I realized what was happening. I know it doesn't excuse what I've done, but I have an idea of how to get her out of there."

Jennifer didn't want to hear her idea; she never wanted to hear her talk again.

Tyler, however, had a different approach. "What are you thinking?"

Rowen's voice had softened, but she spoke quickly and with confidence. "Right now, there's only me and one other person assigned to her. I can distract him long enough to get her out of there. He thinks I'm running down another lead."

Jennifer interjected. "By lead, you mean another family member of ours?"

Rowen didn't answer the question. "The problem is, it can't raise too many suspicions. By suspicions, I mean two guys in dark suits, wearing sunglasses, pulling up to her apartment in a black SUV and escorting her from the building. Lark has eyes and ears everywhere. Just because we're the only ones actively watching, doesn't mean that he doesn't have witnesses. He has a way of getting information."

"You want us to trust you? We don't even know what side you're actually on. How do we know you aren't playing us right this minute?" Jennifer wanted answers, and she was going to get them.

"I want these assholes caught just as much as you do."

Jennifer pushed her finger into Rowen's chest. "I seriously doubt that." She turned to look at Brooke and Tyler. "I say we sit her next to that bag of shit and figure this out ourselves. Then we can ship her back to her own goddamned country." She motioned at Rezentes, who glared at her. "She hasn't been honest with us from the start, and we can't mess with the lives of the people we love by trusting her."

Tyler and Brooke looked at Rowen, waiting for her to answer.

Rowen ran her hand through her hair and took a deep breath. "They came after my kid."

"What? Suddenly you have a child? You have to be kidding me." Jennifer watched Rowen's facial expression change from frustrated to sad.

"It's true. His name is Simon, and he's only three years old. I had been assigned by my government to spy on Lark, and the mission was straightforward enough, until the day I received a package on my doorstep. There were pictures of my son being taken to school, pictures of us together, and a picture of his favorite stuffed elephant sitting in his room. The picture was taken from *inside* our home." Her voice trailed off a bit as she replayed this part of the memory. "It also had a note inside. It said that I was to continue with what I was doing, but in addition, I would also be assigned to follow each of you and report back to Lark's organization. I wasn't to tell my handlers or anyone else, and if I did, they would take Simon. I agreed, always with the intention of getting to the bottom of this and getting rid of Lark. The night you all showed up at the vacated compound, I had called in your arrival well before, long enough for it to clear out. I was watching you, and I was purposely caught by you. I needed to be able to talk to you about what was going on, but I had to make them think I'd been caught, so it didn't look like I'd come to you on my own. I didn't tell you everything because I couldn't jeopardize my son's life." She looked at Jen and gave her a small, apologetic smile. "But I can see that was a stupid thing to do."

Brooke gripped the top of a chair. "If this is all true, where is your son now? What about your husband?"

Rowen put her elbows on her knees and her head in her hands. "No husband. Simon has another mother. My wife went missing almost eleven months ago. She worked for the intelligence agency as well, but she had left when Simon was born. We were on holiday here in the United States when she disappeared. We were spending the day at Six Flags. She went to the bathroom and never came back."

"Didn't you look for her?" Brooke asked.

Rowen shot her a disbelieving look. "Of course I looked for her. I called your police department and tried to file a missing person report. But that's not how it works. There was no sign of a struggle, no clear indication she had been taken, so to them she wasn't missing. I called in every favor that was ever owed me, but no one knew anything. There were no leads, there was nowhere for me to look, and believe me, I tried. But I know for a fact she would have never left Simon. Our son was her entire life, her reason for living. I know I wasn't always the best partner, or the best wife, but she would have never left him. I'd also just started working for Lark, and I'm not convinced he doesn't have her. At first I thought he would tell me, use her as leverage, but now I wonder if he does have her and is using her as a backup plan of some kind. In case I did manage to completely safeguard my son, there was always my wife. I don't know. It all blends together when you've been trying to figure it out as long as I have."

Jennifer felt sorry for her. Rowen was broken because someone had taken a sledgehammer to her life. "Where's Simon, now?"

"He's with a very good friend of mine. He's safe, I call and check weekly."

Tyler sat in front of Rowen. "We can talk more about other things later. Right now, we need to focus. How do we get Jennifer's sister out?"

Rowen thought for a moment, glancing up at the screens. "It needs to be visible and undeniable. There needs to be proof beyond a shadow of a doubt that we had nothing to do with any of this."

"We're listening," Tyler said.

Rowen sat at one of the computer stations and started typing furiously. Images of cars and resorts appeared and disappeared from the screen. Next, she logged into a variety of radio station servers, typing code after code. "Your sister tries to win contests on this radio station every day. I've only been following her for a brief period of time, but it's in the notes. So you need to trust me."

She picked up the phone, and a few moments later started speaking to the person on the other end of the line. She explained that her resort wanted to offer an all-inclusive getaway for the weekend. The radio station didn't have to be convinced to participate, even when she said she wanted it offered in the four-to-five slot this afternoon.

As soon as she hung up, she called the resort, pretending to be from the radio station. She explained that she had just booked the room for the giveaway and again, outlined the details. The resort, like the radio station, didn't require any convincing. And why would they? It was all paid for and would be a good way to get their name out there.

"How do you know they'll pick her?" Tyler asked.

Rowen continued to type. "Because that's what I told the computer to do. The system is going to ignore the other callers and intercept only her sister's. People calling will get an automated response. The station will still receive multiple calls, but they'll all be her sister's line. There's no way she can't win."

"Unless she doesn't call in today," Jennifer added.

"She will call in; she always does," Rowen assured her.

Jennifer felt a twinge of jealousy. She knew Rowen had probably just saved her sister, but she also was jealous that Rowen knew these intimate details about her younger sibling.

Rowen looked at Tyler. "The trip includes limo transportation. Send someone to pick her and her boyfriend up. Lark will send someone to follow, but it will only be one car, easy to lose. By the time they realize what happened and that she's gone, it won't matter. She'll be safe."

Tyler smiled. "It's a good plan."

Rowen smiled back. "I know."

Tyler's smile quickly disappeared. "Now we need to figure out what we're going to do about Caden and about him." She pointed to Rezentes.

Brooke spoke. "We can't turn him in yet. We don't know who else he's working with. Any information that gets out could very well risk Rowen's son and Caden."

Tyler walked over, cupped his chin, and pulled the tape off his mouth. "You're going to tell us what's going on and you're going to do it now."

He held her eye contact, but his voice betrayed him. When he finally spoke, it was shaking. "I'm not telling you anything."

Tyler stared at him for a moment and then pulled out her gun, holding it by her side. "You sure about that?"

If it had been any other day, under any other circumstances, Jennifer would have been sure that Tyler wouldn't have used the weapon in her hand. But right now, she wasn't sure.

"You're going to shoot me?" His eyes got wide.

"I may be doing you a favor, since you're undoubtedly going to be tried for treason. Do you know what that means? You're going to be thrown in some tiny little cell for the rest of your natural life, or sent somewhere as bleak as Guantanamo Bay. So you have two choices. I can shoot you and inflict enough pain to get you to talk…or you can tell us what's going on and maybe they'll show you a bit of mercy. Hell, they might even let you out of your cell for an hour a day to see the sun."

He seemed to contemplate his decision. Tyler's hand moved, and she took aim at his groin. "We'll start low and work our way up."

"I don't know anything!" he shouted, fear cracking his voice. "All I do is report what we're doing and do what I'm told to do. That's it. I swear to God, I don't know anything else."

Tyler continued to hold her gun in place. Rezentes was crying, snot running from his nose, and his shoulders heaving. "You're pathetic." She pulled up a chair and looked down at him, gun still in hand. "What does Carol O'Brien have to do with all of this?"

"All she has ever asked is about our progress with Lark. She wants updates constantly. I don't know about any of her plans."

"Bullshit. I don't believe you would be working with her unless you understood exactly what she wanted. You're too nosy and too narcissistic to operate under a blanket of mystery."

He glared at her, anger in his eyes. They should have burned red with the amount of heat he was portraying in his stare. "All I know is that she promised me a top position in the White House when the task was completed."

"What task?"

"I don't know."

Jennifer cleared her throat to get their attention. "He said you were on his payroll. That you agreed with his mission."

He glared at her from across the room. "I know O'Brien believes in purity, and I'm good with that. I'd be fine with not having a bunch of dykes working for me." He whimpered slightly when Tyler nudged his forehead with her gun. "But I don't know what they're planning. I swear. I was just told to wait until the task was done."

She stood now, her presence looming over him. Her hand flexed on the gun. "What task, Rezentes?"

"All I know is that it would put her in power. Enough power to end all your careers, enough power to let her do whatever she wanted."

"The power of the president?"

He spit on the floor, his eyes not completely dry of tears. "Is there anything greater?"

"Now you're going to tell me everything. How it started, how she approached you, everything."

Jennifer finally felt as though she could breathe again. Her friends had come through, just as she should have trusted them to do when everything had gone wrong in the first place. She watched as Tyler began careful questioning, and Brooke turned on the recorder to make sure they got everything he said on tape.

She turned to her own computer to start entering location data and glanced at Rowen, who was watching Tyler and Rezentes closely. She looked at Jen and gave her a small nod before returning her attention to the discussion. Jen wondered if Caden had slept with her, and if so, if Rowen felt responsible for Caden's arrest. Anger flared again, and she tamped it down. *Focus. Get Caden back, then be mad at them both.* The thought made her smile slightly and she started typing.

CHAPTER TWENTY

It hadn't taken Caden long to realize she wasn't being transported to a typical holding cell. They weren't going to CIA, Homeland, or any other government headquarters. They were heading into the forest. The fact that they hadn't blindfolded her suggested they weren't worried about what she saw, and she knew what that meant. They had no intention of ever letting her go. They intended for her to die here.

Rocks and dust flew in every direction as they flew down the dirt road. It took different twists and turns, the driver following a path he must have taken a thousand times before, since there were no markers, and no obvious indications of where they should be traveling. Caden was careful to count the turns and the time that lapsed in between. She wanted to be sure she could find her way back if, by some miracle, she found her way out. Caden watched his face in the rearview mirror, from the backseat. He never looked back, didn't acknowledge her presence.

"You guys taking me to your secret fishing hole?" She knew she wasn't going to get any straight answers out of them, so she thought if she could get some obscure answers, she might be able to piece a few things together. "Not much for talking huh?"

"Shut up."

"Do you guys have anything to drink up there? I didn't get a chance to grab my juice on the way out."

Again, no answer.

"Come on, guys. It's pretty obvious what you have planned for me. I mean, you didn't even bother to blindfold me. I know when I'm beat. The least you can do is have a conversation with me."

The man in the passenger seat glanced back at her. "We're almost there."

"Almost where?"

"We'll be the ones asking the questions."

"We'll see."

The guy snorted. "Arrogant woman. You have no idea how little you know."

Caden smiled. "How long do you think it will take for them to realize I wasn't actually arrested? You do realize that you just kidnapped a federal agent, right? You call me arrogant? Pssht. You two are going to spend the rest of your lives in jail."

"Sacrifices must be made."

"That's a pretty tag line for a cult. Do you have that on shirts or anything? Can I pick one up in a gift store on my way out?"

The man in the passenger seat turned around to look at her. He calmly slipped his gun from the holster and pointed it at Caden. "You talk too much. Be quiet, or I'll silence you myself."

Caden sat back in her seat. Even she knew which lines shouldn't be crossed, and she had just reached theirs.

The car slowed and pulled up to a large ramp that vanished into the underbrush. The wall at the end of the ramp shifted, sliding open. The car moved down the ramp and into the darkness. Caden closed her eyes against the disappearing sky, summoning the only picture that brought her any solace. An image of Jen soothed her racing heart.

CHAPTER TWENTY-ONE

Deputy Director Martin stared at them. His expression wore the shock that they had already had the opportunity to work past. Rezentes sat in the corner, handcuffed, staring at the ground.

"So, you've come to the conclusion that Lark is working with Carol O'Brien. That there might be a plot to take down the president and the vice president, and somehow Special Agent Styles will be framed for these crimes. Additionally, Mandy Glass, who happens to be Analyst Glass's sister, is being followed for the sole purpose of controlling Analyst Glass. But you've manipulated a radio station giveaway to get her out of harm's way. Additionally, Ryan Rezentes is an informant you have in custody, and Agent Knight is also being used by Lark's organization, who say they'll hurt her son, and might have taken her wife. This possibly even reaches the international level, involving alt-right movements in other countries, who are trying to gain global power. Did I get all of that?"

Tyler knew it sounded crazy when she had spelled it out for him, and now that he had broken it down in such simplistic terms it sounded even more ludicrous. "Sir, I know it sounds ridiculous, but this is what has happened."

Martin raised his hand. "It does sound ridiculous. It also seems completely feasible. We've known there was a mole in the agency, and it sounds like there are probably several. What I need to know now is what we're planning to do about it. Carol O'Brien isn't someone you can just take into custody. She would slip out of that so fast, the next time we all saw each other it would be in the unemployment line. That is, assuming we weren't tossed in jail."

Tyler took a deep breath before she started. "I've reached out to every major organization within the government, and no one has Styles in their custody. I think Lark and O'Brien have her."

He rubbed his face. "I assume you want to go in and get her?"

Tyler took a deep breath and put her hands on her knees. "Jennifer has been able to piece together how far she believes his base to be using a variety of markers. She was blindfolded when she was taken out of the facility, but believes she can determine about how far the location is based on her sense of time and direction. She's also used the rootkit information and pings to get a smaller geographic location on the final stop for the cyber activity. Additionally, we know it's in a heavily wooded location. Glass saw a forest outside the window of Lark's office when he took her. We're running satellite imagery right now, trying to nail down the location a bit more accurately. I know it isn't a lot, but it's all we have right now."

"We've been running satellite imagery for months and have found nothing. Why would this time be any different?" Martin asked.

Jennifer spoke up. "There is another option."

Tyler crossed her arms, disagreeing. But Jen had Martin's attention. "Rowen and I could infiltrate. We've both already had contact with the organization. They believe they have the upper hand with me and that Rowen is working for them. We might be able to get enough information to implicate O'Brien in all of this and find Special Agent Styles at the same time. At the very least, we'll have a starting place and can possibly detain more of Lark's people."

"I don't think it's a good idea, sir," Tyler argued. "We can implicate O'Brien with Rezentes. That will be enough. Analyst Glass is an excellent agent, but she's not a field agent. And Rowen..." Tyler shrugged slightly. "We don't know how much they know about what she's told us."

Jennifer fired back. "As soon as they figure out we know Rezentes is working with them, they're going to be in the wind again. That doesn't give us much time, since he'll be missing from briefings, not answering phone calls and emails. Someone is going to figure it out, and the information will get back. We can't take that chance. They wanted me for something. They wouldn't have brought me in otherwise and told me to wait for further instructions. I think I know now what those instructions will be. It would make sense to have me plant electronic evidence implicating both Knight and Styles in whatever illegal activity they choose. I know it seems a little farfetched, but it's the only thing that makes sense. They thought Rowen was sleeping with Caden, as a way into the agency. If they've taken Caden, that means they don't trust Rowen anymore."

Tyler couldn't think of a reasonable response. She hadn't been able to the last time Jennifer had proposed the plan. So instead, she simply stated her biggest concern. "Glass, you aren't trained to handle the kind of military personnel that you're going to encounter and might have to deal with in a hostile environment. You're an analyst, not a field agent, and there's a big damn difference."

"I'll be with her," Rowen said.

Tyler huffed. "No offense, but I can't trust you with her life. Hell, I don't trust you period."

"You don't have a choice." Rowen met Tyler's eyes. "I explained my side of things. Now you have to take the leap of faith."

The deputy director let out a long breath. "I understand your concerns, Monroe, but I think Glass and Knight are right in this instance. They should go in. You can trail behind at a distance with a team, ready to extract or provide backup when the moment comes."

"Sir—"

He held up his hand. "We have to tread lightly, Special Agent. We can't risk losing them again. Especially if their end game is to eliminate or replace both the president and the vice president. As far as Rezentes is concerned, I'll have him placed in holding with the FBI under another name until this is over. Then he'll be prosecuted for everything he's done." He went over to where Rezentes was sitting. "If you have anything to add that can help, I would suggest you tell us now. It could mean the difference between life in prison and the death penalty." He pulled the tape from Rezentes mouth.

He started to cry again, his shoulders bouncing with each sob. "I've already told you everything I know." His stomach quivered, straining against the buttons that held the material closed on his midsection. "When we caught Glass watching us in the parking lot, I had no idea they were going to pick up Styles too. It wasn't until I got the text this morning telling me to have Glass manufacture evidence against Styles that I understood what was happening."

"Can you still get in contact with her?" Tyler asked, ignoring all his excuses.

He sniffled. "Yes. I can text her."

Martin looked at her. "What are you thinking?"

Tyler tapped her lip with her finger. "He has to assume by now we figured out that the agents who picked up Styles weren't legit. I would've checked on it as soon as she was arrested. He wants us to know he has her; he wants us to know he can get to any one of us at any time. He also thinks he has Glass right where he wants her and that we have no idea. We need Rezentes to get the ball rolling. Have him text O'Brien and tell her the message has been passed along to Glass and she's working on it. Lark doesn't realize we're on to all of this, that we're finally a step ahead. We can let him think Glass is working to frame Styles and we're all running scared trying to figure out how to get her back. Lure them into a false sense of security. It's everything they want to hear so it shouldn't take much."

"Not a bad idea, Special Agent, not a bad idea at all," Martin added.

Brooke turned around and faced all of them. "You're all forgetting one very important piece. We need a more precise location for Lark. We need to make sure we have him in custody before we can secure Caden. If this goes sideways and he's not at the compound, it could get her killed and we could lose him."

Martin nodded his agreement.

Tyler looked at her, a jolt running through her as her mind synced up to Brooke's thought process. There was only one person that could give them the final piece of information they needed to pinpoint Lark's location. She hadn't wanted to go to him until now, unsure if he had informants inside the prison he was being held in. But now there was no other option. Hopefully, they could get to Lark before the information could possibly get back to him. They needed to talk to his son, Chris Carlson. "I'll drive."

❖

Caden put her head down on the table in front of her. She had been in the small room for almost two hours. She understood the game; they wanted to make her wait, wanted to put her on edge. They wanted her to comply. Comply with what, she wasn't all that sure yet. She mentally berated herself for not asking to see their badges right there on the spot. She'd always thought it ridiculous when people said, "It happened so fast," but now she knew what they meant. The only people that had any reason to question her arrest were the people she had been sitting at the table with. No one else knew who she was in that coffee shop, and taking someone in broad daylight in front of people under the guise of arrest was smarter than trying to toss her into a van.

She closed her eyes. She was going to remain calm, collected. She had something that no one else in this facility had. She had Tyler, Brooke, Rowen, and Jennifer on her side. She knew they wouldn't stop until they figured out what was going on and a way to get her out. Now, she needed to do her part. She needed to discover all that she could, so when she did finally get out of here, Lark would be in front of her, handcuffs securely around his wrists.

The door finally opened, and a rather short man entered the room. He was wearing a very expensive suit, far too formal for their current setting. *That's clearly someone who's compensating.* Caden almost smiled. Insecurities could easily be manipulated.

"How is your day going, Ms. Styles?"

Caden lifted her wrists. They still had the plastic ties in place. "I've had better days."

The man pulled out a pocketknife and cut the ties off. "I'm so sorry. Those should have been removed a long time ago." He pulled out the other chair in the room and took a seat. "I'm Nathaniel Lark. It's nice to meet you."

Caden purposely controlled her facial response. She had spent a year looking for the person who was now sitting only a foot away, introducing himself like they were at a dinner party. She had never been able to put a face to his name, and now here he was. She looked at him for a moment before she answered. She wanted to make sure her voice wouldn't vibrate with the rage she felt gushing through her body. "I'm Caden Styles. But you already knew that."

He laughed. "I did. But, all the same, it's still very nice to meet you. I've been keeping tabs on you for so long, I feel a bit starstruck."

This guy was certifiable. "You could have come down to my office whenever you felt like it. I would've loved to have met you sooner."

"Well, I appreciate the flattery, but we both know that's not true. You want nothing more than to see me sitting behind bars."

Caden shook her head emphatically, purposely dramatic. "Not true. I want nothing more than to see you sitting in the electric chair."

His eyes widened at her simple statement. She was telling the truth and he knew it. "And here I thought we were going to be friends. I've spent so many months watching you and your little friends. I've been tracking you, your progress, your patterns. You've all gotten so close to meeting me in person so many times. But here we sit, you on one side of the table and me on the other. But it's you that came in wearing the restraints."

"For now."

He smiled. "Caden. Can I call you Caden?" He didn't wait for a response before he continued. "You have devised a plan to assassinate both the president and the vice president of the United States. If anyone is going to be sitting in the electric chair, it's going to be you, my friend."

"That's absurd. What could I possibly have to gain from that? No one will believe you. I've been tracking you for a year. Do you honestly think anyone will believe that I have also been secretly plotting to destroy the upper levels of government? Please. You should have thought this through a little better. This has Lark written all over it."

"I like you. You have so much fire in you, self-assurance. Do you know how rare it is to find someone that is so married to their convictions? Well, let me tell you, it is. It's a very admirable trait, Caden. I'm sure your parents are very proud of you. I wonder what they'll think when this news breaks." He widened his mouth in a faux surprised look.

"You do understand that the people you sent to pick me up aren't real agents, right? There is absolutely no evidence to support anything you're saying. I hate to tell you this, but in this country, you need evidence to convict someone."

"Do you? That's where you are mistaken, my friend. Most people are tried in the court of public opinion, in this day and age. People will assume your guilt or innocence long before you ever see the inside of a court room."

"You're implying this would ever see the inside of a court room. You've created a bullshit reality, where you come out on top. That's not how this story ends."

He smiled. He reached into the bag he had brought in with him and pulled out a laptop. A few clicks later, he turned the screen around. "I even had someone put it into a PowerPoint for you. Isn't that cool?"

He flipped through the images. Rowen and Caden filled most of them. Shots of them together walking, talking, even in her apartment sharing their one and only kiss. Her skin crawled. She was about to protest that this proved nothing. He held up a finger before she said anything. He pushed the play button and a sound clip started playing. She recognized Rowen's voice. She was talking to a man whose voice she couldn't place. The agreement they made boiled down to one point—she would assist in an assassination. Although it was unclear who the target was intended to be.

"That still doesn't prove anything. I kissed her and was in a few pictures with her. That doesn't automatically make me an accessory."

He smiled as he clicked the button and the next image appeared. It was a small boy, being carried into a building. The woman holding him was Rowen.

He tapped on the screen. "That little guy right there, that's her son. Well, I guess it's her partner's son. I'm not sure exactly how to define everything in your little dyke world. The point is, how far do you think she would go to protect that little boy? Do you think she would spend her life in prison? Do you think she would implicate you, someone she barely knows, in something?"

He clicked another button, activating yet another sound bite. It was Caden and Rowen having a conversation that never took place. It was her voice, agreeing to help Rowen with whatever she needed, no matter the cost. "That never happened."

He laughed. "I know! Your adorable friend Jennifer put it together for us. She sent it over to me not even an hour ago. She's very talented, don't you think?" He closed the computer, still smiling. "Isn't this fun? It didn't even take that much convincing. All we had to do was threaten her little sister." He sighed. "See, this is what's wrong with all of you. You leave yourselves so open to attacks by caring about people, trusting people, wanting to protect people. It makes you all weak."

Caden's head was spinning. It was difficult to process everything she was hearing. She knew her hands were shaking; she felt her whole body tremble. She had no resolve left to stop it. Rowen had been playing them, well, she'd been playing Caden, this whole time. And there wasn't anything Jennifer wouldn't do to protect her sister. It all made so much sense. Everyone had to protect someone else, and if that meant leaving Caden in the wind, so be it. No one was close enough to her to care about what happened to her. Everything became crystal clear in that moment. Caden ran over to the corner of the room and vomited into the trashcan.

He started patting her back. "You know, I never wanted it to come to this. It's you that made it personal."

"What are you talking about?"

"My son. He's going to spend the rest of his life behind bars. You remember Chris, don't you? He would have made a fine CIA analyst. And if it had been him on the inside, I would have never needed Jennifer. I could have done all of this without having to threaten her or her sister. It all comes full circle, doesn't it?"

"Chris Carlson made his decision when he turned on us. And it's your fault he's sitting behind bars. You sent him in to do your bidding and he got caught. It's not our fault he wasn't any good at playing double agent."

His grip tightened around her shoulder. "You, Monroe, Glass, Hart, you all made a career out of catching him. Every one of you is where you are now because of what you did to him."

She pushed him off and took a step backward. "You and Carlson are guilty of treason, and you will both pay for it with your lives."

He smiled at her. "No, Caden, *you* will pay for it. Either that, or Jennifer's sister and Rowen's kid will die." He smiled. "See, now we really *are* having fun."

She wiped her mouth with the back of her hand. "What exactly are you proposing, my life for theirs?"

"Caden, I don't want you to just blindly take blame for an assassination attempt. I want you to take credit for the *actual* assassination of both the president and vice president." He looked down at his watch. "Either way, they'll both be dead in about eight hours. What you need to decide is whether or not Mandy Glass and Simon Knight will also be dead. If you take the blame, we've got no further use for them and they're home free. Obviously, that won't happen until the needle is in your arm, but it will happen. Or you can fight this, make a ruckus, and have innocent blood on your hands. We'll still win, I assure you. But your life will be ruined regardless. See? You've got a choice. Easy peasy."

CHAPTER TWENTY-TWO

Y ou should let me do the talking." Brooke gave Tyler a sideways glance.

Tyler chewed on her bottom lip. "I don't really want you going in there at all."

"It's a good thing you aren't my boss then."

Brooke's phone buzzed and she read the text. "Jen sent the clip to Lark over the message wire."

Tyler took a deep breath, looking both anxious and relieved. "Good."

The guard came into view first. He unlocked the heavy metal door and slid it to the side. A few moments later, the prisoner entered the room. The bright orange jumpsuit he wore plainly identified him as a criminal. His shackles clattered as he walked into the room. He saw Brooke first and smiled. Next, he glanced at Tyler and the smile just as quickly disappeared.

He took a seat at the metal table, his handcuffs scraping across the top. His hair was completely gone, shaved all the way down. He had gotten bigger since the last time Brooke had seen him, his muscular frame forged by the months spent behind bars. Brooke knew he was in solitary confinement, considered too much of a national security risk to be allowed with the rest of the inmates. Not that there were a significant number in this location. It was in an undisclosed area, underground, and the general public had no knowledge of its existence, much less its occupants.

"Hi, Chris."

"Brooke." He smiled and looked at Tyler. "Gunnery Sergeant."

"How are you?" Brooke asked.

He looked around the cell and at the four guards that stood behind him. "It's a regular party here." He smiled at her. "You look great." She felt her body shiver, and Tyler shifted next to her, clearly not liking his comment or the way his eyes were raking over her.

"We need your help." She wanted to get to the point. He was intelligent enough to have infiltrated the CIA, fooling everyone he had come into contact with. He had trained for deceit and manipulation his whole life, so concise questions and answers were the only viable approach. At one time, he had been her teammate, and she often wondered where he would be if it weren't for his bloodline, something he had no control over.

He focused on only her. "I can't imagine what I can do for you."

"We need to find Lark." She wouldn't use the term father. If there was any chance they were going to get the information they needed, she wanted to insinuate that she saw them as different people, different entities.

"You waited a long time to come and ask me. Why now?"

Brooke wanted to say it was because she didn't trust him. She didn't know how far Lark's reach went. That if she had come and spoken with him earlier, if any of them had, the information could have gotten back to his father and he would have moved again. But now, it didn't matter. They'd get him no matter what. But with Chris's help, they might find him faster, and that could mean the difference between life and death for Caden. Instead of saying any of that, she played the sympathy card. "I wanted to give you a chance to heal, to feel better."

He snorted. "You always did look out for me."

Brooke nodded. "I tried." Brooke knew he had a small crush on her while they were at the Farm together, and she was counting on that now to dull his senses a bit.

"What's in it for me?"

Tyler straightened. "A chance to do the right thing. The opportunity to redeem yourself, even if no one else ever finds out that you helped. It's your chance to be the man Brooke thought you were."

He watched them both, looking into each of their eyes with different degrees of loathing and longing. "You really can't find him, can you." It wasn't a question. He was stating a fact.

"I can see what I can do about getting you a bit more time outside."

His eyes were fixated on her lips as she spoke. The lust she saw burning in his eyes made her skin crawl.

"I want you to come here once a month and eat dinner with me."

"No. Absolutely not." Tyler's voice was adamant, final.

Brooke couldn't look at her. She had no resolve when she looked into those blue eyes. No ability to answer his question, the way she knew it needed to be answered. "Okay."

The look of satisfaction that crossed his face was both sinister and triumphant. Brooke suppressed the shiver that rippled under her skin. She had no intention of honoring this commitment, but she couldn't let him know that, and she didn't even want him to consider it.

He smiled broadly and motioned for the pad of paper sitting in front of Tyler. "I'll tell you exactly how to get there."

❖

Rowen hung up the phone and smiled at Jennifer. "Your sister is safe and sound. A team just picked her and her boyfriend up. Everything went just as planned."

Jennifer let out a breath she had been holding for the last several minutes. "Thank you for that."

Rowen looked at her with kindness in her eyes. "Sure."

Jennifer watched her move around the room, checking different monitors. She allowed herself to consider the information Rowen had divulged earlier about her family. She wanted to know more. She wanted to know more because she wanted to trust her.

Jennifer pushed a pen back and forth on the desk. "Where is he? Your son."

Rowen turned halfway around and gave a small smile. "He's with a friend of mine, back home in France. My cover is that I'm in the military and she believes I'm deployed. Which, as far as cover stories go, is pretty close to the truth."

Jennifer didn't need to ask about parents or siblings. The family Rowen had described was all she had. She knew because she could recognize the loneliness and heartbreak. She felt it herself.

"We have to get her back." When Jennifer said it, it was almost a whisper.

Rowen nodded. There was an unspoken understanding that she was referring to Caden. Jennifer wasn't sure how things were going to turn out between the two of them, but she knew her world was a better place because Caden was in it.

"We will. I promise."

Jennifer knew that Rowen meant it. She could hear it in her voice.

"Do you love her?" Rowen asked.

"Do I love Caden Styles? No. She drives me absolutely crazy. She is a womanizer, arrogant, selfish, and at times, obnoxious."

"But you could."

Jennifer felt her chest burn with the answer. "Yes, it would be very easy to love her."

"Yes, it would."

Jennifer watched Rowen's face. She braced herself for a surge of jealousy, but one never came. Her face didn't hold any challenge; she was being honest and sympathetic. They had a shared view of Caden. They saw goodness that bubbled underneath the rough exterior. Jennifer could almost consider them being together if they got out of this. *Almost. Just give me the chance to try.*

CHAPTER TWENTY-THREE

Tyler pulled on her Kevlar vest and adjusted the sides, making sure it was snug against her body. Next, she checked her sidearm and ammunition. She pulled the rifle from the storage locker and checked the sight. She could feel Brooke's eyes on her, but even if Brooke hadn't been standing right next to her, she would have been aware of her presence. Their connection tethered Tyler to her safe place. There was nothing she valued more, needed more. She lived for the moments she spent in Brooke's arms. That tether would always bring her home. She would fight any enemy, climb any barrier, and beat any enemy to get back to her.

When she had all her equipment in order, she turned to Brooke, who fell into her almost instantly. She wrapped her arms around her and buried her face in her shoulder. "I love you. I need you to be safe. I need you to come home to me."

Tyler kissed the top of her head. "I'll always come home to you."

"Promise me."

"I promise."

Brooke pulled her head down and drew her in. Their kiss was filled with passion, promise, and just as it always was, a bit of wonder. "I don't know what I would do without you."

"Don't worry about things that will never come to fruition." Tyler kissed her again. "You aren't getting rid of me that easily."

Tyler's radio crackled. "Red team, ready."

She answered, not able to quite take her eyes off Brooke yet. "Roger that. Two minutes."

Brooke hugged her. "I'll be in headquarters and in your ear."

"I wouldn't have it any other way."

❖

Caden had spent the last several hours weighing her options. Sure, he took her in broad daylight, but the only person who would think to look into it was Tyler. No one else in that diner knew who she was and whether or not she should have been arrested. She had to admit, Lark's plan was brilliant. He had accounted for nearly everything. He didn't know what they knew, and that was the only thing working in their favor. The team knew that Carol O'Brien was the one calling the shots. His arrogance also allowed him to forget one very important thing—the only way his plan worked was if the president and vice president were *both* killed. He had shown his cards too early. His need to brag about his accomplishments had opened him up to his biggest vulnerability. That, and he didn't know Tyler Monroe. Not if he believed that he outsmarted her. If he really believed she hadn't figured out what was going on yet, he was going to be in for a big surprise.

She needed a plan, and letting Lark and O'Brien get away with it wasn't on the list. Lark wanted the world to think she was conspiring to kill the two most powerful people in the world. In order to do that, he would need to have his hands off the button altogether. She started pacing around the room; movement always helped her to think. Then it came to her—he was trying to lay the groundwork to make the world believe that she ran this organization. Her stomach tightened. She felt sick all over again.

She assumed the team was coming, but she couldn't bet her life that they would get to her in time. Hell, they didn't even know where she was exactly. Escaping was at the forefront of her mind, and it could be a plausible option, although the chance of getting out would be slim. *What do I really have to lose?* At this point, they weren't checking on her at regular intervals, but when they did, they were in pairs. She could handle two at a time. Each of the guards carried an M-16 rifle, which meant she would have at least two in her possession as well as a radio. That was as good a start as any. Even if she didn't make it out alive, she would take as many down with her as possible, so the team wouldn't have so many to deal with when they made it through.

Caden was aware of the lone camera in the corner, meant to keep an eye on her. She moved around the room, wanting to keep up the façade that she was simply pacing. After a few moments, she slumped down the side of the wall. She couldn't be sure, but she hoped her feet were still visible for the camera, giving the appearance that she was resting. She slid off her belt and wrapped it around her hand. It wasn't much, but the metal might be enough to pack a little extra "umpf" when she got the opportunity to throw a punch. *I may only get one shot.*

She focused on her breathing, wanting to calm her senses and help make her more aware. She closed her eyes and listened to every noise she could, hoping to anticipate footsteps or chatter from the hallways. Hell, even hearing the closing or opening of a door would be beneficial. An unbidden image of Jennifer came to mind, and her breath caught. *If I get out of this, I'm going to get her to talk to me. I need to tell her...* Tell her what? She didn't know, but she knew she wanted to make things right. *Whatever that means.*

❖

The SUV came to a silent stop a half a mile from their target. Tyler hopped out of the vehicle, five team members following right behind her. They had gone over the plan, and they were going to stay in tight formation. The primary objective was to procure Caden. After that, another six teams would infiltrate the camp. Lark would become the one and only target. She already knew that Carol O'Brien wasn't inside the walls. She was attending a state dinner with the president, the perfect alibi.

Tyler flipped her night vision goggles into place, and her team fell in behind her in pairs. "Control, red team."

"Go ahead, red team."

"Moving into position."

"Copy that, red team. Kill radio chatter unless necessary."

"Roger that."

Tyler moved forward into the darkness. The team's footsteps were virtually silent as they moved along the dirt path that led to a tunnel. The tunnel was right where Chris had said it would be, and she was grateful that at least in this instance, he had told the truth.

Tyler ducked behind one of the trees to the left of the ramp that led underground. She scanned the upper levels, looking for a camera. The camera was right where she thought it would be, turned toward the entrance. She also knew that there would be dozens more inside the facility. Once they disabled the security cameras, the whole facility would know someone was there.

She pulled out the trigger box from her right pocket. The blue team had placed a series of small mines a quarter mile in front of the facility's entrance. The trigger would activate the mines and send a majority of the security force to the front of the building. That would give her team approximately seven minutes to get inside and find Caden. She pushed the trigger, and a few moments later, a series of loud popping noises permeated the air. The ground shook slightly. Tyler hit the timer on her watch and moved down the ramp toward the door.

She motioned to the door, and one of the team members came to the front. He placed a small packet of C4 on the handle and stepped back. A loud pop sounded, and he pulled the door from its hinges.

The tunnel floor was nothing more than dirt paths. The lights flashed orange and red, indicating their admittance into the facility. Tyler ducked behind the first alcove, and her team followed. She motioned for them to break into three teams and move down the hallway. They knew the drill; this is what they trained for.

Tyler moved first, making it almost ten steps before a guard came around the corner. She and her teammate ducked into a doorway, knowing the other four behind her would do the same thing. She reached into her pocket and pulled out a flash grenade, pulled the first and second safety pins with her teeth, and heaved it down the hallway. The clanging of the flashbang hitting the ground was first, followed by the distinctive boom and a blinding flash of light. The grenade wasn't lethal, but it would disorient anyone in the premises. Gunshots fired down the corridor in their direction, blindly strewn at the people he knew were there. His shots were high, intentionally aiming for heads and torsos he couldn't see. Tyler crouched down and slid out from behind the doorway. He came into vision, and she took her shot. His body hit the ground only a second later.

There would be more and they needed to move quickly. Adrenaline pumped through her. It felt like molten liquid in her veins; her hands were tingling, but her breathing was controlled and quiet. She moved past the body, kicking the gun away. She purposely didn't look at his face. She never did. The pain and heartbreak that always came after having to kill someone was what her nightmares were forged from. She knew this night would be another in the long index of demons she would need to conquer, but it came down to her friend or them. The answer was simple.

CHAPTER TWENTY-FOUR

Jennifer and Rowen sat in the immaculately decorated office. Jennifer stared at the same paintings she had seen just days before. This time, a different feeling burned in her stomach. The images of fire, anger, and destruction made her think of where she wanted to send Lark when this was all over.

He sat in his chair, elbows on his desk, two fingers in a peak over his mouth. "You two have discovered one another, I see."

Rowen, looking as relaxed as ever with her hands folded in her lap, smiled. "That is what you wanted, isn't it? For us to figure out exactly how far your reach was capable."

He smiled, his oddly handsome face beaming with arrogance. "Yes, I guess it was. Though of course, you still have no idea."

Jennifer stared at the radio on his desk. She wanted to grab it and smack him in the face with it. Caden was somewhere in this facility, and she had no idea if she was okay, what they had done to her, and if that damage would be reparable. The longing for Caden that had always bubbled under her skin and trickled into her subconscious at inopportune moments was now a raging need that coursed through her blood, quicker with each beat of her heart. She wanted to cause him pain, the same pain that he had inflicted, not just on her friends and family, but the country. She forced herself to look away. "We're here to do whatever you need."

"I'm curious, how exactly did you find this facility?"

Jennifer shrugged. "Isn't that why you wanted me? Because I can do things others can't. I got you what you wanted on Caden. I proved my worth."

He smiled at her, but that smile quickly faded. He was a mad man, but he wasn't stupid. "What do you get out of this?"

"I just want my sister to be safe. I want you to arrange transportation out of the country for us both when you've done whatever it is you needed us for."

He looked at Rowen now. "And what about you?"

"I want what I've always wanted."

"Me too." He reached down and pulled open his drawer. He placed a gun on top of his desk and slid it over to Rowen. "Finish what you were hired to do, Ms. Knight."

Rowen stared at him, and Jennifer stared at her. "What is he talking about?"

Lark laughed and clapped his hands like some creepy psycho child. "She hasn't told you? Oh, she is much more loyal than I ever hoped for."

He turned on the large monitor behind him. It was fuzzy for a moment and then the images came into view. It was a split screen. On the left was a video image of a sleeping little boy whom Jennifer assumed was Rowen's son. He appeared to be about three hundred feet away. The image was focused through a sniper scope. She had told Jennifer he was tucked away at a friend's house, safe. But this image proved her assumption to be wrong, the familiar distance lines that marked the scopes proximity and the look on Rowen's face were all the proof Jennifer needed that these people could reach anyone, anywhere. The right video image was a woman in a cell. She looked tattered, thin, and broken.

Rowen stood, stumbling backward a few steps. Her fists were clenched and her breathing rapid, her eyes fixed on the screen. "You've had Christy this whole time?"

He stood and moved toward her, grabbing the gun off his desk on the way. "Come on, are you really all that surprised? Where did you think she went? She just up and left you and your son? You see, I knew this day would come. I knew that eventually I'd have all of you, right where I wanted you." He pulled a small device out of his pocket. It looked like a pen, but had a tiny red button on top and a matching green button on the bottom. "If I push the red button, they die; the green one, they live. I have two, one for each. In case you were getting any fancy ideas about trying to save them both and killing me. It's just not going to happen. Now, kill her so we can continue with our evening."

Rowen took the gun from his hand and aimed it at Jennifer. Jennifer got out of her seat and put her hands in the air. Her heart was thumping so loudly in her ears she was sure everyone could hear it. Bile rose from her stomach up through her throat. She had never considered that terror might have a color but it did. It was bright white, and it started to burn hot in the peripheral vision. "Rowen, you don't have to do this."

Lark laughed from behind his desk. "Yes, she does. Your little friend here is my secret weapon. I'm going to use her to kill you, Hart, and finally Monroe. In a perfect world, Monroe would be here to watch you go first, but such is life. She'll have to miss this one. You gave me what I needed to deal with Styles, and you're no longer of any use to me. But of course, loose ends and all that."

Jennifer ignored him and talked to Rowen. "Rowen, if you do this, will you be able to look your son or Christy in the eye ever again?"

Rowen had tears streaming down her cheeks. Her hand was shaking, but the gun remained trained on Jennifer. "No. But they'll be alive and they can be together."

"You don't really think he's going to let you go after this?"

"It doesn't matter. I have to try to save them. I'm sorry."

Jennifer heard the popping noises, and then a rumble shook the room. At first, she thought Rowen had pulled the trigger and that she had been shot. The lights flickered and Lark came running out from behind the desk.

"What the fuck?" he yelled as he grabbed the rifle from behind the desk and moved toward the door.

Tyler. Tyler was on her way. All Jen could do now was hope and pray that she would get here in time. She knew the first objective was to get Lark and then to find Caden. And for whatever reason, in that split second she was okay with the order of the mission objectives. As long as Caden got out safely, this wouldn't be in vain. She'd be sorry, though, not to get to look into Caden's eyes one more time.

❖

Tyler and her team took a left at the tee in the hallway. They had already taken out six guards when she heard Brooke's voice in her ear.

"The schematics aren't clear. We only have partial reads from the satellite. But it looks like the concentration of bodies is going to be on your left."

"Copy that." Tyler motioned for them to continue.

The structure of the facility had changed. It was no longer dirt paths and poorly lit hallways. These halls were tiled, well lit, and each door was encased in steel. She moved past each door, peaking into the small window. At the fourth door, she saw a woman, lying on a cot in her cell. She seemed to be unaffected by the flickering lights and loud noises that rumbled through the building. She didn't want to break up her team, she needed every single one of them, but she couldn't take the risk of leaving her in there. If she and her team didn't make it out, at least they had gotten one captive out of the building first. She motioned to two of the members that were bringing up the rear and pointed to the door.

"Get her out and take her to one of the cars. Stay with her."

The shots were becoming more frequent and closer. Tyler hugged her body to the wall, and she continued to move as fast as possible, still checking each of the rooms. Finally, on the last cell before another corridor, she peered into the window and saw Caden. Before her team could get the C4 in place to blow the door, two guards came running down the hallway, guns blazing.

The first two shots missed, the bullets landing somewhere behind her. One of her teammates screamed a profanity and disappeared into a doorway, blood smearing across the white tile as he pulled himself out of the way. Tyler shot low, hitting a guard's legs. The second one retreated into a doorway. He turned his weapon out from behind the doorway and fired blindly down the hallway. She made it over to the guard still on the ground who was reaching for his gun. She stepped on his hand and heard the small bones break under the pressure. She took the butt of her gun and smashed the side of his face, rendering him unconscious.

Another shot was fired from the doorway. It sliced through the sleeve of her shirt leaving an opening where the cotton material used to be and blood oozing in its wake. The heat from the bullet seared her skin, but she knew it was only a flesh wound. She ducked behind the doorway, only a few feet from the guard who had just shot her. She saw one of her team members move across the hallway, drawing fire. When the guard took aim, exposing his arm, Tyler fired. The bullet went through his forearm, and he dropped his weapon. She quickly moved to his side, her team covering her. He held his arm, his face bright red, saliva dripping from his nose and mouth. He was going to say something, but Tyler didn't give him the chance. She grabbed his throat and squeezed. His breathing was becoming more labored, his one good hand thumping against her arm. Finally, he passed out.

A loud pop sounded behind her, and the door of Caden's cell came off its hinges. Caden ran out. "Took you long enough."

"I got held up." She slid the gun the guard had been holding across the floor over to Caden.

"You're losing your touch."

Tyler pulled the ammo belt off the guard and slid that over to Caden as well. "You wish."

"Which way to Lark?"

Caden fastened the belt and checked the gun. "I don't know. He didn't exactly give me a tour when I got here."

"Then we'll just have to wait for the signal from Knight and Glass."

Caden's voice was angrier than Tyler expected it to be, given that they had backup inside the facility.

"You shouldn't have let Glass come."

"She's with Knight. She'll be fine." She motioned for two of the team members to fan out. "Keep checking the cells for captives." Caden counted for at least two men, and the relief she felt in having her by her side bolstered her confidence. For the first time since she had entered the facility, she allowed herself to believe they might make it out alive. "Let's go get this bastard, shall we?"

Chapter Twenty-five

The door was locked. Lark yanked on it, shaking the handle. "God damnit!" He ran over to his computer and punched a series of keys. "Fucking panic room bullshit! I can't override this damn thing!"

Jennifer reached down and pushed a button on her watch.

Rowen tightened her grip around the gun. "Don't move."

Lark came back out from behind the desk. He aimed his rifle at the door and pulled the trigger. The first shot echoed, and small pieces of metal flew through the room. The same thing happened with the second shot, then the third. The fourth shot finally blew the handle off the door. Jennifer covered her ears and wanted to move out of the way, but there was nowhere to go. Rowen lunged for Lark, trying to grab the pen, but he was faster. He pushed down on the red button with no remorse in his expression.

Rowen was on her knees, and he turned the rifle on her. "Get me out of here or the kid dies next."

Jennifer watched Rowen's hands tremble as she pushed herself upright and onto her feet. She wasn't sure how Rowen was able to move at all. She assumed Rowen's body was running on some type of autopilot function, created by years of training.

He grabbed Jennifer and put her in front of his rifle, pushing her out the door. He looked at Rowen and motioned for her to get in front, then tossed her a handgun. "Clear the way."

Rowen and Jennifer did as they were told. As they moved down the hallways, Jennifer held her breath as each corner was cleared. The shots were getting louder, and the building continued to shake from explosions. She knew the other teams had arrived and that there would be nothing but chaos and blood the closer they got to an exit, any exit. The likelihood of them being caught up in random crossfire was growing more imminent with each step.

"Make a left!" Lark huddled behind his human shields.

That left turn took them face-to-face with Tyler, Caden, and two men wearing black fatigues and camouflage.

Tyler and Rowen aimed their guns at one another.

"Get out of the way!" Rowen yelled at them. The relief Jennifer felt at seeing Caden's face was quickly eclipsed by her hopes of them listening to Rowen. They had no way to know that her son's life was being threatened, and Jennifer knew no loosely hinged friendship would prevent her from protecting him.

"Put the gun down, Knight," Tyler yelled back. Tyler and Caden knelt down, took aim, and one of the team members behind them backed up their stance, while the last turned and covered them from behind.

"Who do you think is faster, Monroe? Do you think you can get your shot off before I kill her?" He shoved Jennifer forward next to Rowen.

She watched Caden's and Tyler's eyes as they focused their weapons. They didn't have a shot and they knew it. Lark was completely shielded behind Rowen and her. They would have to shoot them to get to him.

Jennifer didn't realize she had been crying until she tasted the salty liquid on her lips. She knew Tyler and Caden would never shoot her. Instinctively, she knew that either one of them would offer their life for her own, but that was the last thing she wanted. Taking out Lark meant saving the president and vice president, and possibly protecting the world from foreign organizations that could be combining their efforts. It meant he wouldn't be out there hurting people any longer. If she had to die for that, so be it. At least she'd been able to see Caden one more time. She let moments flash through her subconscious, moments she would have done things differently. She would have been a better daughter, a better sister. She should have forgiven her father, not because he deserved it, but because she did. She would have taken a chance with Caden, outcome be damned. A broken heart from Caden would at least be proof she had lived.

❖

Caden's hand tightened around the grip of her gun. The tears that fell from Jennifer's cheeks were like knives cutting across her skin. They weren't going to be able to hit him from here, not without hurting Rowen and Jennifer. And hurting Jennifer wasn't something she could bear, even if Jennifer had sold her out.

"You're surrounded, Lark. Put down your weapon," Tyler yelled, never moving her weapon.

"Move aside or they die."

"Then you are going to have to kill us all," Tyler yelled back.

Shots echoed behind them and Caden said, "We need to fall back. They're coming from behind and we'll get pinned between them."

Tyler's frustration was clear, her teeth gritted, and Caden watched her jaw clench. She slowly stood, and they moved backward until they were in another corridor and out of sight.

More gunshots sounded at the other end of the hall, and Tyler ordered the red team to hold them off. Caden watched as Lark came into view once again, turned down the opposite hallway and headed toward the exit. He was walking backward, still holding Rowen and Jennifer in front of him. Moving together, Caden and Tyler followed him toward the exit.

Caden was willing Jennifer to fall, to lie down. Anything that would afford them a clean shot.

When they reached the door, Lark pushed Rowen forward. "Kill them."

Rowen lifted her weapon and aimed it at Caden. "I'm sorry, but he'll kill my son."

Suddenly, Jennifer jerked loose from Lark, shoved Lark's rifle upward, and then slammed into Rowen, sending them both crashing into the wall and then to the floor as they struggled with Rowen's gun.

Lark turned and ran. Caden and Tyler took off in a dead sprint, passing Rowen and Jennifer. Caden thought briefly about stopping to check on Jennifer, but she couldn't leave Tyler without backup. Surely, now that Rowen wasn't under his gun, she wouldn't hurt Jen. She would be there to help her. Lark went up the ramp and turned left, his expression full of panic. He ran backward for a moment, firing at them. The bullets missed, kicking up dirt as they hit the ground. He was almost to the Jeep when Tyler knelt down and pulled her rifle up to her face as Caden trained her 9mm on the man they'd been hunting for too long.

But before either of them could pull the trigger, a loud popping sound came from their right, and Lark fell to the ground, door to the Jeep already open. Tyler stood and ran toward Lark; Caden took off in the direction of the gunshots.

The sound of sirens filled the forest. The loud whines of emergency vehicles and various law enforcement agencies with their red and white lights that illuminated the darkened area were a welcomed sight.

Tyler finished placing the handcuffs on Lark and flipped him over. She ignored the open wound in his shoulder and the blood that slid from his body into the dirt, as well as his moans of pain.

She grabbed the small device in his hand, a light on each side, one red and one green. She examined it and pulled it open. It was an empty tube, the lights were dummy switches, attached to nothing. She put it in her pocket, figuring she'd work out what he was using it for later. "You're going to be tried for treason, and I'm going to be there when they put the needle in your arm."

He spit at her feet, blood dripping from his mouth. "I've always had an ace in my pocket. I'll never see a cell."

She smiled down at him. "You mean O'Brien? We already know."

His eyes bulged and the veins in his neck popped out, fear radiating off him. "You won't get her without me. Not for everything. And there's so much more you don't know."

The paramedics ran over with a gurney and started working on him. She unlocked his handcuffs and reattached them to the bed once they'd placed him on the gurney. They pushed him into the ambulance, and Tyler instructed two of her team members to ride with him and not to let him out of their sight. He kept yelling at her, telling her she'd have no choice but to cut him a deal, that he had friends in high places. Clichés from a bad guy that made Tyler smile.

"See you soon, Lark."

As soon as the ambulance was gone, she radioed in to headquarters. "Control, Team Leader."

Brooke answered, and hearing the familiar tone was the last piece of the puzzle to put Tyler at ease. "Go ahead, Team Leader."

Tyler smiled. Just hearing Brooke's voice warmed her chest. "Lark is on his way to the hospital. ETA thirty-six minutes. He's in one of the traceable vehicles. You can confirm his location."

Tyler could hear the smile in Brooke's voice. But she could also hear the worry. Brooke would know about the flesh wound on her arm, having been privy to the operation through the cameras on their helmets. She wouldn't be fully settled until she could inspect her for herself.

"Roger that. Come in for debrief when the area is clear."

❖

Caden got to the ridge and took cover behind a tree. She got low and looked beyond it. A blond woman had her gun pointed at two agents lying on the ground, unmoving. Caden yelled, keeping her back against the tree. "Homeland Security. Put your weapon on the ground."

The woman dropped her weapon, seeming to be pulled from a daze. She held up her hands, and the terrified look in her eyes told Caden she wasn't a threat. She lowered her gun but kept an eye on her.

"I didn't mean to hurt them." The woman pointed to the two agents who were now pushing themselves up off the ground. "They helped get me out of there, but then they tried to shove me in a car, and I just couldn't...I couldn't be confined like that again."

Caden recognized the two men as part of Tyler's team and was a little surprised this scared woman had overpowered them both. The woman must have seen the confusion on her face because she answered Caden's unasked question. "When they tried to push me in the car, I managed to get one of their guns away, and they lay down voluntarily." She then reached down on the ground, grabbed both the men's radios, and handed them to Caden. "I'm sorry."

Caden handed them back to the agents, who looked a bit sheepish.

"Is he dead?" the woman asked.

"I don't know. But that was a hell of a shot. Who are you with?"

"My wife, my son, do you know if they're okay?"

"I don't know. I'll help you find out, though. What's your name?"

"Christy. Christy Knight. I'm part of French Intelligence, or at least I was. I retired a while back."

That explains being able to get the agents on the ground. Caden helped her over to the backseat of the car and radioed for a medic. "Any relation to Rowen Knight?"

The woman looked up at her. Her eyes filled with tears, and she grasped Caden's arm. "Do you know where she is?"

Caden patted her hand. "Yeah, I do. She just tried to kill me."

CHAPTER TWENTY-SIX

Jennifer watched as Rowen ran to the arms of the woman she had only moments ago believed was dead. She kissed her cheeks, and they knelt together in the dirt, holding one another and sobbing. It was impossible not to be moved by the scene. Her own emotions bubbled close to the surface. They ranged from aggression to gratitude. So many things had transpired in the last few hours, it was hard to rein in what she was feeling and identify it in easy, concise terms. Fear for her sister, Caden, and herself had been shredding her nerves, and now that it was over, she wasn't sure how to process everything she had felt in such a brief period of time.

"How are you?" Caden's presence was a welcome reprieve from her swirling thoughts.

"I've had better days." She turned and rested her head against Caden's neck. Feeling her arms around her was the only thing she wanted. The strength and assurance that she needed was found in that simple caress.

"You saved me back there," Caden murmured against Jennifer's hair. "When Lark played that recording you made, I thought maybe you'd really betrayed me. But when I saw you in that hallway, I realized you'd never do that. Instead, you put your life on the line."

Jennifer sniffled and she gripped Caden tighter. "You would've done it for me."

Caden kissed the top of her head. "There isn't a whole lot I wouldn't do for you."

"Will you take me out on a real date?"

"I don't know about that."

Jennifer shoved her chest. "You're such a jerk."

"Usually." She laughed and pulled Jennifer close again. "You know I'd love to."

Tyler came toward them, her rifle held across her chest. "We need to get back. This isn't over."

"You know," Caden said, "as far as bosses go, you aren't my favorite."

Tyler pushed past them both and climbed into the SUV. "Yes, I am."

❖

Headquarters was a hive of controlled chaos. Orders that had been dropped from the upper levels had everyone running in circles. Each person seemed to believe their order was more important than the next. The president and vice president had been secured into their respective bunkers, and the hunt for information on foreign contacts was in full force.

The one person no one could find was Carol O'Brien. She had been placed on the "No Fly" list hours before, the streets had been shut down, and there were agents searching for her. Still, it was as if she had vanished.

Brooke was aware of what was going on around her. She could hear all the talking, the shouting, and in some instances, even accusations. People were discussing how far the corruption reached and who was responsible. She heard it all, but her eyes remained fixed on the set of monitors that would show Tyler coming back to headquarters.

Finally, the string of SUVs filed into the garage. Brooke ran down the steps, not bothering with the elevators. They were filled with too many government employees, too many people that had just recently become aware of the mission and now were in full swing.

Brooke had been able to watch everything that happened. She was able to feel as if she were a part of the pursuit and capture, but she hadn't been physically there, and now she needed to touch Tyler. She needed to see and feel for herself that she was okay.

She made it down to the garage just as they were all exiting the vans. Tyler, who always seemed able to sense her presence, turned when she got out, meeting her eyes. Brooke didn't run to meet her, that would seem ridiculous to everyone around, and she knew they had to stay professional. Still, with every normal step she took, her body wanted to fling itself into Tyler's arms.

Tyler led them into a hallway off to the side, and Brooke gave in to her need to feel Tyler against her. She grabbed her and held her in her arms. She squeezed, breathing her in, and she could taste the salt and dirt on Tyler's skin. It was a taste Brooke had learned to love. This wasn't the first time they had hidden in this very hallway, holding each other, in this very position.

"You got him," Brooke breathed into Tyler's neck.

"We got him." She kissed the top of her forehead.

"I wasn't sure how this would play out for a bit."

Tyler laughed. "You doubted me?"

Brooke shook her head. "No, never. I doubted my resolve to watch it come together."

"I'll always come back to you."

Brooke pulled away and checked Tyler's arm. The hole where the bullet had grazed her was now covered in dried blood, dirt, and sweat. It was bruising and red, pus still oozing from small breaks in the wound. "You need to get this looked at."

"I'm fine."

Brooke took her hand and pulled her down the hallway. "You need stitches. Stop being stubborn." Tyler would be fine, but Brooke needed to take care of her, to feel in control, even over something so simple. It was difficult to be away from Tyler when she was out risking her life, and it was even harder to watch. But Brooke knew it was nothing compared to what some significant others had to endure, not knowing for hours, if not days, what was taking place.

"Did they get O'Brien?"

Brooke didn't slow her pace toward the medical unit. "No."

Tyler stopped and pulled her hand away. "We need to go get her. We need to stop her before she manages to find a way out of the country. We need—"

Brooke cut her off. "You need stitches. You need to take a deep breath. You need to let other people do their jobs."

Tyler glared at her. Brooke knew Tyler was mulling over the words in her head, deciding an appropriate reaction. "We can't let her get away."

"I know. We won't. But it's not just us working on it anymore, babe."

Tyler's dedication to duty was something that Brooke loved and respected about her. The flip side of that coin was that she put the mission before herself. Brooke, on the other hand, was always acutely aware of how vulnerable Tyler was, and the superficial wound on her arm was a reminder of that. Every time Tyler left the protective confines of her arms, Brooke never knew if she would return. This time it had worked out in their favor, but Brooke never knew if the next time would be different. This possibility always gnawed at Brooke's insides and was only extinguished in these moments right after Tyler's return. The moment when Brooke could touch her and know she was safe.

❖

People were running around the control room, everyone moving in a different direction at speeds that weren't conducive to an office space. Caden stood with her arms crossed, people scurrying around her, on their phones, pulling up satellite images; unit commanders were barking orders.

She looked at Jennifer. "What a shit show."

Jennifer nodded. "This is what happens when other units aren't filled in and everyone finds out at once."

"It looks like they're pulling every agent, manager, and director in for questioning."

"They are."

"Good."

Tyler walked in, picking at the bandage on her arm. Brooke was right behind her, and she swatted at Tyler's hand, telling her to stop.

"What do we know?" Tyler asked.

Caden pointed at her arm, and Tyler shooed her motion away. Caden knew if Tyler was seriously injured, Brooke wouldn't have let her back in control, regardless of what the doctors had said. Relieved, she focused her attention back on the computer screens. "Well, the entire city is shut down. Every airport in a hundred-mile radius is grounded. But we can't keep it like this forever."

Tyler nodded. "She has the means and the connections to stay hidden until the coast is clear."

Jennifer snorted. "The coast is never clear when you try to kill the president and vice president."

Caden didn't agree. "The coast will always clear when you have enough money."

Deputy Director Martin came into the room. He looked around for a moment before seeing the four of them standing together. He motioned and they followed him into a meeting room.

He closed the door behind them. "You did great. Actually, you did outstanding. I need written reports from all of you, debriefing the events as you saw them, but after that, I want you to go home. If we have any follow-up questions, we'll contact you. Take a day off and I will see you Monday. Hart, Glass, you too."

Tyler stepped forward. "Sir, with all due respect—"

He held his hand up. "I know what you're going to say, Monroe, so don't. There is nothing any of you can do right now. We've taken all necessary precautions to stop O'Brien. We have Lark and every person under his direction from the compound in custody. We have combined efforts with several law enforcement agencies, and we're moving on mobile outposts as we speak, thanks to some very chatty detainees. Come back in on Monday and we'll get back to work. You all need some sleep, food, and a shower. We have everything under control here." He gestured to the commotion behind them. "I'll call you if there is anything you should know or if there's anything you can help with. And before you argue, I'm ordering, not asking."

Caden wasn't sure if he would answer the question, but she had to ask. "What about Rowen and Christy Knight?"

He looked at her for a long moment, pursing his lips. "They're being handed over to the French government. Part of the agreement we made with them upon having Knight work with us was that she would answer to their government and their government alone. They will be here in the States for the next twenty-four hours, awaiting transport."

"Where are they being held?"

"Special Agent Styles, you know as well as I do that I'm not permitted to give you that type of information. But we are keeping them safe and close at hand. They'll have all the privacy and security they need. Go home. Rest. You deserve it." He left the room, his instructions clear.

Caden watched him leave, grateful for the information. He wouldn't come out and tell her, but he might as well have. They were downstairs, in the same holding area they had kept Rowen in when she first arrived. It was the most secure location available, and he wouldn't have entrusted their safety to another law enforcement agency, nor would he risk placing them somewhere like a hotel.

Tyler looked at her. "I'll go with you."

Brooke put her hand on Tyler's arm. Caden, who was normally put off by any public displays of affection, even small gestures, caught herself looking. For the first time, she wished for that type of connection. She was jealous, not of either of them particularly, but of what they shared. She had felt it when Jennifer had fallen into her arms at the compound, the blatant need to feel the warmth of someone who cared about you and needed your presence. What she didn't know is if the feeling could be replicated, even with Jennifer's request for a date. It was a far stretch from what Tyler and Brooke shared, but she was willing to try.

"I'll take Jennifer home after she finishes her report and meet you after. Please don't be too long."

"I won't," Tyler promised.

Caden didn't know she was going to say it, but the words left her mouth before she had a chance to stop herself. "I'll only be a few minutes with Rowen. If you don't mind waiting for me, I'll take you home, Jen."

Jennifer looked at her for a long moment, probably weighing the sincerity of her offer, based on her reputation and all that had happened between them. "I'd like that, thank you."

Caden was both surprised and excited. She wasn't sure what Jennifer's reaction would be, but being open to the idea of Caden taking her home was exhilarating.

❖

Caden and Tyler walked down the halls, glancing into the small windows of each of the cells they passed. After four rooms, they found the right one and Caden pulled out her security card, pressed it against the monitor outside the door, and then pushed it open.

Once they were both inside, Caden realized she wasn't entirely sure what she wanted to say. There had been an attraction between her and Rowen, but now she looked at the two of them, sitting on a cot, holding each other, and she felt nothing but relief. She was glad Rowen had found Christy and happy they would be able to return to their son. Christy had no visible physical wounds, but the mental lesions of being captive for so long would never fully heal.

Caden looked at Christy. "How are you?" Caden had originally considered posing the question of Christy's well-being to Rowen first. She didn't want to startle her, she was clearly overwhelmed, but she wanted her to feel like a person who deserved to be addressed directly.

Christy looked up at her and gave a half smile. "I'm okay, thank you."

"I don't know if anyone has told you or not, but we got him. He'll never see the light of day. We couldn't have done it without you. If it weren't for your shot, he might have made it into that Jeep and gotten away."

"Thank you for saying that."

Rowen took a step toward Caden. "Caden, we should talk."

Caden shook her head. "There's nothing to say. I just wanted to come down here and thank Christy personally and wish you both the best."

Rowen didn't owe her an explanation and there was nothing for them to hash out. They'd both been doing their jobs, and sometimes shit got messy when that happened. Rowen had her wife back now. Whatever fleeting attraction they had, it didn't matter. They had only shared a single kiss, but even if it had been more, Rowen was exactly where she needed to be.

"Just so you know, I wouldn't have pulled the trigger. I need you to know that. I would have figured out something, even if

Jennifer hadn't made her move. And I had no idea they were going to pin all that shit on you. I would have told you, if I'd known. I swear." She swallowed and looked at her wife before looking back at Caden and Tyler. "Anyway. Take care of yourself, Caden. And, Tyler, be good to Brooke."

Tyler surprised Caden by wrapping Rowen in a hug. "Take care of yourself, Rowen. I can't imagine what you've gone through, and I don't think any one of us would have done anything differently from what you did. Brooke taught me that forgiving yourself is hard, but damn worth it. Give it a try."

Caden smiled at them again, hoping she was able to communicate her genuine happiness for them being together again. She glanced over at Tyler. "Let's give them some space." At the door, she looked back at Rowen. "Good luck."

"Thanks."

They made their way down the hallway in comfortable silence. For the first time in weeks, maybe even months, Caden felt hopeful. She was excited to see Jennifer. Even if nothing ever came of it, she was going to give it a shot. The prospect alone made her hopeful and left her feeling energized.

Chapter Twenty-seven

Tyler took the steps to her apartment two at a time. The need to see Brooke was just as strong as when they had first met. She opened the door and felt the tension of the day melt away. Candles were placed in different locations all over the apartment, casting flickering shadows across the room. The smell of vanilla and cinnamon warmed her chest and gave her the familiar sense of home.

She walked into their bedroom and dropped her bag at the door. There was a note on the bed. *Take a shower. I'll be back in a few. Love you. XOXOXOXOXO.* Tyler smiled and peeled off her clothes. She dropped them into the hamper and stepped into the shower. She turned on the spray and let it wash over her body. She used to pray to whatever higher power would listen that the shower would pull the nightmares and regrets down the drain. Now, since Brooke, she saw it for what it was, cleansing. All the pain, hatred, and death they faced every day could be defeated. There was beauty, loyalty, and love. Those were the things worth fighting for, worth giving your life for. She would gladly take the balance. She could handle whatever was out there waiting in the shadows because with Brooke, she felt like she stood in the light.

She stepped out of the shower and found Brooke sitting on the bed, smiling. Her brown hair fell at her shoulders and her green eyes danced in the candlelight. She was everything Tyler had ever wanted and a thousand things she never knew she needed.

"Where did you go?"

"I went to get champagne, to celebrate."

"What are we celebrating?"

Brooke pushed herself off the bed and went to her. She wrapped her arms around her neck and kissed her chin. "Everything."

"I can get behind that."

"I figured you could."

Brooke ran her hand over Tyler's arm. Her face looked pained as she reached the spot the bullet had grazed her. "How does it feel to have Lark in custody?"

Tyler smiled at the words. *Lark in custody.* "It feels amazing, but it also feels a little surreal. I never thought we would be here. I mean, we aren't quite done, not until O'Brien is sitting in a hole somewhere, but I'm going to enjoy this moment for what it is, a victory."

"We'll get her." Brooke leaned over and kissed Tyler's shoulder.

Tyler leaned her head against Brooke's. "I'm proud of you."

Brooke looked up at her, her eyes showing the very beginning stages of arousal. "Of me? For what?"

Tyler focused on what she wanted to say before she gave in to Brooke's draw. "Well, normally, we wouldn't be sitting here with champagne. I'd be sitting in a hospital room somewhere getting an X-ray on my arm. You'd be listing off the reasons we should let the FBI or someone else go after O'Brien."

Brooke kissed below Tyler's ear. "I'm working on my control issues. I want you to be who you are, even when I can't control the outcome."

Tyler squeezed her eyes shut, allowing Brooke's words to wash over her body. "How much control are you willing to give up?"

Brooke pushed Tyler backward on the bed and climbed on top of her. She grabbed her hands and pinned them down. "Oh, I'm not giving up all my control."

Brooke's mouth moved down Tyler's neck and onto her chest. "I was hoping you would say that."

❖

Jennifer sat in her living room, watching as Caden moved from picture to picture on her wall. The ride to her place had been spent discussing trivial topics. They discussed the unseasonably warm weather, a local band they both enjoyed, and whether or not Caden should purchase a new tablet. Jennifer knew Caden well enough to know she had been nervous, but what she couldn't figure out was why. They had spent hours together. Hell, they had spent a night in bed together, and now Caden was acting like they were on a first date of sorts, just getting to know one another.

"Caden, you've looked at those pictures at least a dozen times. What's going on?"

Caden put her hands in her pockets and rocked her weight back and forth. "I just don't want to screw anything up."

That wasn't the response Jennifer had been expecting. She had expected a deflection of some kind, not a blatantly true statement. She decided if Caden was going to be utterly honest, she would be as well. "What are you worried about screwing up?"

Caden came and sat on the couch next to her. She chewed on her lip for a moment. "I'm not really an expert at this whole dating thing. I can talk you into bed, but I don't know how to do this." She pointed between them.

"Believe it or not, I'm not an expert at dating either."

Caden took her hand and rubbed her thumb over the top. "I can't begin to tell you how scared I was that I might lose you."

The honesty in her voice made Jennifer's heart skip. "I was scared too. I don't think I have ever been so scared."

"I'm sorry. It must have been categorically terrifying for you. You aren't used to those situations, and I can't begin to imagine how you—"

Jennifer kissed her. Listening to Caden try to understand her point of view and her pain was too much. She needed Caden to understand that the fear she felt wasn't for herself but for Caden's well-being. She didn't know how to explain it, so she hoped the kiss would explain everything.

Jennifer put everything she had felt into the kiss. Every moment she felt that she might never see Caden again. Every guttural memory of what it felt like to be in her arms. Every moment she was able to make it through because the possibility of being in her arms again was still out there, almost close enough to touch.

Caden pulled at her until she was finally in her lap. The intensity of their kiss continued to climb until Caden finally pulled away. She leaned her head against Jennifer, catching her breath. "Wow." She kissed Jennifer's cheek. "I don't think I have any other words for that."

Jennifer ran her hands up and down Caden's arms. They were firm, strong, and she wanted them around her. She kissed her again. She felt Caden lean into her, her hands under her shirt, running up and down her back. It wasn't the most sexual experience she had ever had with Caden, but it was the most intimate.

Again, Caden stopped their forward progress. She slid out from underneath Jennifer and stood. Her face was flushed and her hands were trembling. She leaned down and kissed the top of her head, holding her position for several moments.

"Where could you possibly be going?" Jennifer didn't understand what was happening. The last thing she wanted was for Caden to walk out the door.

"I want to do this the right way." Caden leaned down again and kissed her cheek. "I don't want this to be like all the others. I'm going to take you on a proper date."

"What?" Jennifer couldn't believe what she was hearing. Caden Styles, the queen of the womanizers, the master of aloofness, wanted to make sure they went out on a proper date before they had sex again. Or could it be that she didn't really want Jennifer at all and she was trying to back out as quickly and easily as possible? "Look, Caden, if you don't want this, have the decency to say that."

Caden's eyes got big, and she shook her head vehemently. "No! That's not it at all. I've never wanted anything more than I want this. I just want to take things slow, make sure we do it right. I want you to feel as special as I know you are."

Jennifer's chest tightened. She had never seen this side of Caden. She was sincere and vulnerable. It was sexy and sweet. "Okay."

"Okay?"

Jennifer wrapped her arms around Caden and looked into her dark brown eyes. Her light brown skin still wore the blush of their kisses. Her full lips were parted, starting to turn up in a smile. Jennifer kissed her cheek. "Take me on a date. I would like that."

Caden put her head against Jennifer's and whispered, "Wednesday night?"

"Sounds perfect."

Caden let her go and moved toward the door. She was beaming with excitement. "I'll see you then."

Jennifer stopped her before she left. "Caden?"

She turned and looked at her. "Yeah?"

"I'll actually see you Monday. You know, at work."

Caden stumbled over the doorstep. "Yeah, that's right. See you Monday."

The door closed, and Jennifer fell back onto the couch. She couldn't remember ever feeling like this before, and the bliss made her giggle. She felt like a teenager, and it was wonderful.

Suddenly, she couldn't wait to get back to work. This time, the desire to be there had nothing to do with wanting to avoid her life or the voids in it and everything to do with a person that might fill in those missing pieces. Someone who had been in front of her all this time. It was time to let go and trust. Caden wanted her, and that was a hell of a start.

CHAPTER TWENTY-EIGHT

W here are you taking Jennifer to dinner?"

"What?" Caden knew Tyler had said something, but she wasn't sure what. She had been having trouble really focusing since last seeing Jennifer. The high she was feeling was never something she had been able to reach with any substance or any woman.

"Where? Where are you taking her?"

Caden turned in her chair to look at Tyler. "Why does it matter? And how do you even know?"

"It matters, and Brooke." Tyler gave her a knowing nod.

"Since when are you the expert on women? Pretty sure that's my area of expertise." Caden was reluctant to tell Tyler just how nervous she was about this date. The teasing that would ensue wasn't worth any amount of insight Tyler might be able to give her.

Tyler laughed. "Getting them in bed, sure. Convincing them to like you, not so much."

"Everyone likes me."

"Well, we both know that's not true."

"Shut up."

Deputy Director Martin sat down at the table. Caden hadn't heard him come in and felt foolish for having this conversation in front of him. She glared at Tyler, who just looked away and tried not to laugh.

He sat at the table and sipped his coffee. "Take her some-where nice, Styles. If you really like her, don't skimp on the first date."

Caden wanted to disappear into her chair.

Tyler hit her arm and pointed at Martin. "See."

Caden gave her a dirty look. "Thanks, guru of love."

The phone rang and Martin picked it up. "Yes, send him in."

A few moments later, another man entered the room. His suit was impeccable, perfectly creased, and pinstriped. He nodded at Tyler and Caden and shook Martin's hand.

"Special Agents, this is the new Department of Defense Intelligence Officer, Captain Calvin Hart."

Caden's ears were hot. She wanted to say what popped into her head, but luckily, she knew *holy hell* wasn't the appropriate thing to say.

"Happy to be here." He said it, but that's not what his ex-pression indicated. He looked a little uncomfortable.

"He has been briefed and will be assisting overseeing the apprehension of Carol O'Brien. He has requested that you two be assigned to the task force."

"Needless to say, I was very impressed with the mission you two not only oversaw but took part in. We need you on our team." His stare lingered just a moment longer on Tyler than it did on Caden, though he made no reference to the fact that he knew her.

Tyler, who normally would have been popping to attention in her normal military way, said nothing, and Caden knew her well enough to know she was contemplating what this new de-velopment meant.

Caden looked between the two men, wanting to break the awkward moment. "When do we start?"

Martin took another sip of his coffee. "I'm reassigning you until this is over. You're now at the Department of Defense's bid-ding. Do us proud."

Captain Hart got up and motioned for Tyler and Caden to follow. Once they were in the hallway, he turned and faced them. He stared at Caden and then focused his attention on Tyler. "I meant what I said in there. I was impressed with how you performed. I'm looking forward to working with you."

Tyler held her head up a bit higher. "Here to serve, sir."

He smiled and started toward the door. "Good, then follow me. We have a lot of work to do. Carol O'Brien is on her way to Dubai, and I need you two to apprehend or eliminate her."

Tyler followed him down the hallway, her new mission objective turning over in her mind. She glanced over at Caden and allowed herself a moment to reflect on how different her life was now than when she had walked down a similarly lit hallway on her way to teach her first class at the Farm. She had better friends than she could've ever imagined. She had a true partner in Brooke, a connection that would stand up to any test and against any opposition. For the first time in her life, she was complete. She wasn't sure what the next mission had in store for her team, but she knew they would make it through together.

About the Author

Jackie D was born and raised in the San Francisco, East Bay Area of California. She now resides in Central Pennsylvania with her wife and their numerous furry companions. She earned a bachelor's degree in recreation administration and a dual master's degree in management and public administration. She is a Navy veteran and served in Operation Iraqi Freedom as a flight deck director, onboard the *USS Abraham Lincoln*.

She spends her free time with her wife, friends, family, and their incredibly needy dogs. She enjoys playing golf but is resigned to the fact she would equally enjoy any sport where drinking beer is encouraged during game play. Her first book, *Infiltration*, was a finalist for a Lambda Literary Award.

Jackie can be reached at:
Email: Jackie_d1981@yahoo.com
Facebook: facebook.com/jackied.lesfic.author
Website: www. jackied-author.com

Books Available from Bold Strokes Books

Complications by MJ Williamz. Two women battle for the heart of one. (978-1-62639-769-9)

Crossing the Wide Forever by Missouri Vaun. As Cody Walsh and Lillie Ellis face the perils of the untamed West, they discover that love's uncharted frontier isn't for the weak in spirit or the faint of heart. (978-1-62639-851-1)

Fake It Till You Make It by M. Ullrich. Lies will lead to trouble, but can they lead to love? (978-1-62639-923-5)

Girls Next Door by Sandy Lowe and Stacia Seaman eds. Bestselling romance authors tell it from the heart—sexy, romantic stories of falling for the girls next door. (978-1-62639-916-7)

Pursuit by Jackie D. The pursuit of the most dangerous terrorist in America will crack the lines of friendship and love, and not everyone will make it out under the weight of duty and service. (978-1-62639-903-7)

Shameless by Brit Ryder. Confident Emery Pearson knows exactly what she's looking for in a no-strings-attached hookup, but can a spontaneous interlude open her heart to more? (978-1-63555-006-1)

The Practitioner by Ronica Black. Sometimes love comes calling whether you're ready for it or not. (978-1-62639-948-8)

Unlikely Match by Fiona Riley. When an ambitious PR exec and her super-rich coding geek-girl client fall in love, they learn that giving something up may be the only way to have everything. (978-1-62639-891-7)

Where Love Leads by Erin McKenzie. A high school counselor and the mom of her new student bond in support of the troubled girl, never expecting deeper feelings to emerge, testing the boundaries of their relationship. (978-1-62639-991-4)

Forsaken Trust by Meredith Doench. When four women are murdered, Agent Luce Hansen must regain trust in her most valuable investigative tool—herself—to catch the killer. (978-1-62639-737-8)

Her Best Friend's Sister by Meghan O'Brien. For fifteen years, Claire Barker has nursed a massive crush on her best friend's older sister. What happens when all her wildest fantasies come true? (978-1-62639-861-0)

Letter of the Law by Carsen Taite. Will federal prosecutor Bianca Cruz take a chance at love with horse breeder Jade Vargas, whose dark family ties threaten everything Bianca has worked to protect—including her child? (978-1-62639-750-7)

New Life by Jan Gayle. Trigena and Karrie are having a baby, but the stress of becoming a mother and the impact on their relationship might be too much for Trigena. (978-1-62639-878-8)

Royal Rebel by Jenny Frame. Charity director Lennox King sees through the party girl image Princess Roza has cultivated, but will Lennox's past indiscretions and Roza's responsibilities make their love impossible? (978-1-62639-893-1)

Unbroken by Donna K. Ford. When Kayla and Jackie, two women with every reason to reject Happy Ever After, fall in love, will they have the courage to overcome their pasts and rewrite their stories? (978-1-62639-921-1)

Where the Light Glows by Dena Blake. Mel Thomas doesn't realize just how unhappy she is in her marriage until she meets Izzy Calabrese. Will she have the courage to overcome her insecurities and follow her heart? (978-1-62639-958-7)

Escape in Time by Robyn Nyx. Working in the past is hell on your future. (978-1-62639-855-9)

Forget-Me-Not by Kris Bryant. Is love worth walking away from the only life you've ever dreamed of? (978-1-62639-865-8)

Highland Fling by Anna Larner. On vacation in the Scottish Highlands, Eve Eddison falls for the enigmatic forestry officer Moira Burns, despite Eve's best friend's campaign to convince her that Moira will break her heart. (978-1-62639-853-5)

Phoenix Rising by Rebecca Harwell. As Storm's Quarry faces invasion from a powerful neighbor, a mysterious newcomer with powers equal to Nadya's challenges everything she believes about herself and her future. (978-1-62639-913-6)

Soul Survivor by I. Beacham. Sam and Joey have given up on hope, but when fate brings them together it gives them a chance to change each other's life and make dreams come true. (978-1-62639-882-5)

Strawberry Summer by Melissa Brayden. When Margaret Beringer's first love Courtney Carrington returns to their small town, she must grapple with their troubled past and fight the temptation for a very delicious future. (978-1-62639-867-2)

The Girl on the Edge of Summer by J.M. Redmann. Micky Knight accepts two cases, but neither is the easy investigation it appears. The past is never past—and young girls lead complicated, even dangerous lives. (978-1-62639-687-6)

Unknown Horizons by CJ Birch. The moment Lieutenant Alison Ash steps aboard the Persephone, she knows her life will never be the same. (978-1-62639-938-9)

Divided Nation, United Hearts by Yolanda Wallace. In a nation torn in two by a most uncivil war, can love conquer the divide? (978-1-62639-847-4)

Fury's Bridge by Brey Willows. What if your life depended on someone who didn't believe in your existence? (978-1-62639-841-2)

Lightning Strikes by Cass Sellars. When Parker Duncan and Sydney Hyatt's one-night stand turns to more, both women must fight demons past and present to cling to the relationship neither of them thought she wanted. (978-1-62639-956-3)

Love in Disaster by Charlotte Greene. A professor and a celebrity chef are drawn together by chance, but can their attraction survive a natural disaster? (978-1-62639-885-6)

Secret Hearts by Radclyffe. Can two women from different worlds find common ground while fighting their secret desires? (978-1-62639-932-7)

Sins of Our Fathers by A. Rose Mathieu. Solving gruesome murder cases is only one of Elizabeth Campbell's challenges; another is her growing attraction to the female detective who is hell-bent on keeping her client in prison. (978-1-62639-873-3)

The Sniper's Kiss by Justine Saracen. The power of a kiss: it can swell your heart with splendor, declare abject submission, and sometimes blow your brains out. (978-1-62639-839-9)

Troop 18 by Jessica L. Webb. Charged with uncovering the destructive secret that a troop of RCMP cadets has been hiding, Andy must put aside her worries about Kate and uncover the conspiracy before it's too late. (978-1-62639-934-1)

Worthy of Trust and Confidence by Kara A. McLeod. Agent Ryan O'Connor is about to discover the hard way that when you can only handle one type of answer to a question, it really is better not to ask. (978-1-62639-889-4)